SHADOW MAN

Shadow Man

Iron Horse Mystery #2

C.J. Shane

Published by Rope's End Publishing.

ISBN paperback: 978-1-951524-25-8

ISBN e-book: 978-1-951524-26-5

Typesetting services by BOOKOW.COM

Acknowledgments

Sincere thanks go to Tucson graphic designer Lynne East-Itkin for the book cover design, and to Dawn Lewis of County Durham, England, for editorial services.

CONTENTS

1 SUNDAY POTLUCK

Logan Reid stuck tiny candles into several little plastic candle holders, then he carefully placed the candles into the soft surface of the birthday cake resting on his dining room table. He had no idea how old Frida was, but it was her birthday, she was a part of the Casa Pacifica family, and he was determined to provide her and the others with a birthday cake. He'd bought the cake at a nearby bakery earlier that afternoon. When he returned home, he decided to decorate the cake with twelve candles, one for each month. He was pretty sure Frida would like that. Maybe. He guessed maybe she'd like it. He hoped, anyway.

The problem was that Logan had no idea what he was doing. When he was growing up, those birthday cakes always seemed to appear magically, thanks to his mother. And in the years that he was married, his wife Caroline took care of this kind of stuff. But Caroline was gone now, with nothing left but the memory of their lives together and her sudden death. Three and a half years ago.

Logan shook his head. "Stop brooding," he muttered to himself. Life was good, wasn't it? He was manager of the Casa Pacifica Apartments, so his rent was low. He and the tenants had formed a peculiar little family. They helped each other out, and they ate pot luck dinners with each other every Sunday evening. He had his grad-student teaching job at the university, and he was about to get his PhD in May. Best of all, his five-year-old son, Charlie, was healthy and seemed happy most of the time. Logan's life revolved around Charlie.

Suddenly, an image of one of the Casa Pacifica tenants slipped into his consciousness. Zoey Corban. She was sweet and pretty and fun to be around, and she clearly adored Charlie. Logan trusted her, and because of that, he allowed Charlie to go do things with her when Logan wasn't present. After Zoey had traded herself for Charlie so he could escape a crazed killer, Logan trusted her completely with his precious son. Not many people would put themselves under a killer's control so that someone else's child could go free. Logan hoped that Zoey would come to the pot luck and help them all celebrate Frida's birthday.

The door to his apartment flew open, and Charlie ran into the room. Zoey was close behind.

"Daddy, we found some!"

Logan looked up and was pleased to see Zoey grinning at him. He returned her smile. Earlier in the afternoon, she'd come by and asked Charlie if he wanted to go on a "bug hunt." Charlie's enthusiastic response was to jump up and down and squeal, "Yes! A bug hunt! A bug hunt!" They had been gone almost three hours.

"What did you find?" Logan asked.

"Some dragonflies. We took pictures. Zoey said we could collect the dragonflies, but she thinks it's better to just let them live their lives. So Zoey took photos. She's going to share the photos with me. I'm going to make a bug scrapbook."

"So you went to the river?"

"Yes," Zoey said. "Charlie, which river did we visit?"

"The Santa Cruz!" Charlie was dancing around in a circle now. "We saw some Pond Damsel dragonflies that are called American Bluets."

"You're teaching him the correct names?" Logan smiled again at Zoey.

"Definitely. The word 'bug' just won't cut it." Zoey laughed. "I'm a biology teacher at the high school, remember?"

Suddenly Charlie noticed the birthday cake. He approached and stared at it. Then he turned to Logan and asked, "Can I have some cake?"

Logan nodded. "Yes, but this is Frida's birthday cake so we'll have it for dessert this evening. We'll sing 'Happy Birthday,' and she has to blow out the candles first." He looked at Zoey. "I hope you'll come to the potluck this evening."

"I wouldn't miss it for the world." She turned toward the door. "I need to go home and make something to bring to the pot luck."

Charlie ran to her and gave her a big hug. "Thank you for taking me on a bug hunt."

"Thank you for going with me." Zoe grinned. She smoothed down his wayward, tousled blond hair. "We'll do it again sometime."

Charlie started his spins around the room again, singing "Bug hunt! Bug hunt!"

She waved goodbye, and Logan returned the wave. "Thanks, Zoey."

She nodded and closed the door behind her.

"Charlie, bath time."

"Do I have to?"

Logan was always amazed at how Charlie's happy tone could instantly turn into whining when a bath was mentioned. And it was odd how he seemed to enjoy himself once he got into the bath water. Getting there was the problem.

"Yes, you have to take a bath. I can see dried mud on your legs. And hurry up. Everyone will arrive soon."

"Okay. Okay." Charlie sighed and headed toward the bathroom.

"And put those muddy shoes outside the bathroom door. I'll clean them up later."

"Zoey said I need some wading boots."

"Okay. We'll talk about that later. Focus on the bath."

Logan waited until he could hear the bathwater running, then he went to the kitchen to check on a pan of lasagna in the oven. He surprised himself. He was actually starting to like cooking. Sometimes. He heard a soft knock on the door.

"Logan, it's me."

Logan recognized the voice of Cass Cosay who was staying in the apartment on the second floor just above Logan and Charlie's ground floor apartment.

"Come on in."

Cass opened the door and entered. He was carrying a plate of muffins. "I bought some mesquite meal at the San Javier Co-op Farm, and I added it to the muffin recipe. They turned out pretty good. The mesquite gives the muffins a nice, nutty flavor." Cass Cosay was a tall, muscular man, with a reddish-brown complexion that revealed his Apache Native American heritage. His black hair had grown out some, and he wore it in a knot at the back of his head.

Logan took the plate and placed it on the table. "San Javier? That's the Tohono O'odham farm. Thanks for making these muffins. I'm glad you're here because I've been wanting to talk to you about how things are going. I haven't seen much of you lately."

During the altercation with the would-be killer that held Casa Pacifica residents Nina Perry and Zoey Corban as hostages, Cass had revealed to Logan and Canadian visitor Gwilym Havard that he was an FBI agent. Cass took down the villain, disarmed and arrested him, and freed both Zoey and Nina.

"Everything is going well," Cass said. "My team and I were able to identify a group of smugglers and drug dealers working out of Fourth Avenue, quite near here. We made several arrests."

"Smuggling what? Drugs?"

"They were smuggling the chemicals used to make fentanyl pills. The chemicals are imported into Mexico from China. Usually the fentanyl pills are made in Sonora in northern Mexico, then smuggled across the border into the U.S. We're trying to figure out why they've started smuggling the chemicals across the border. We're thinking that they have been manufacturing the drug here as well as in Mexico. We caught them selling the pills, too, and now we're looking for where exactly they made the drug. The fact that they were selling the chemicals here also suggests that there might be other gangs who have entered the market and are making the drug here as well."

"That drug, fentanyl, I mean, scares me to death," Logan said. "It looks like candy."

"Yes. Very dangerous. Kids and teens sometimes think they are eating candy. Death comes really fast."

"I'm glad you arrested a bunch of them. How's it working out for you to live here?"

"Good. This Iron Horse neighborhood is pretty quiet, but it's close enough to all the action so I don't have to go very far to get involved. I like the apartment here, too. It's comfortable, and you and the other tenants are good people. I'm actually thinking about taking a little break from work for a while since we made these arrests. If it's okay, I'd like to continue staying here."

"No problem. Gwilym paid the rent in advance. After what you did, rescuing Nina and Zoey from that nutcase with the gun, you can stay as long as Nina and Gwilym agree. I can't predict really what will happen with them. Nina loves Vancouver, and she loves Gwilym even more. They might come back to Tucson just for visits but live most of the time in B.C." Logan looked into the oven again. "Ten more minutes, I'd say."

"That smells great."

"I also wanted to ask you. Are you keeping it a secret that you're an FBI agent? Earlier, you told Gwilym and me not to mention that to anyone."

"I used to work undercover most of the time so I definitely didn't want anyone to know then that I'm FBI. My job changed over time, and now I'm a Special Agent with other duties. I'm not undercover, and don't plan to be, so my job isn't really a secret now. However, I don't usually advertise what I do. In fact, I stay pretty quiet about it. But, sometimes, I do tell people if they seem okay."

"I think all of us feel safer with you here."

Suddenly a loud voice came from the bathroom. "Daddy! There's something in the water!"

Logan headed for the bathroom. He came back in a few minutes, shaking his head. "Another bug. He's saving it to show to Zoey."

Cass chuckled. "Ah, the important things in life. Bugs in the bathtub."

A series of knocks on Logan's door was followed by the entrance of the other friends, also tenants, in the apartment building. The seven Casa Pacifica apartments were located in what had been a railroad executive's home, built in 1920s in the Spanish Revival style. Later, the apartments were created from the original home. The apartments were spacious, and all had large windows that looked out on the mesquite trees in the side yard and the tree-lined street in the front.

Li arrived next. His real name was Liang, thanks to his Chinese heritage, but Li was easier. He worked as a chef at a leading Chinese restaurant. Zoey, the biology teacher and bug hunter, came next. Then Frida, the birthday girl, arrived. Frida was a bartender who spent most of her free time organizing labor protests. Last to arrive was Dylan, the accountant. The only tenant still missing was Marc, a photojournalist who was on assignment and not currently in Tucson. Each one placed their dishes on the large dining table.

Logan had his lasagna out of the oven now and on a trivet on the table. "I'll set the table. My helper who usually sets the table isn't being very helpful. He's still in the bath." Logan went to fetch plates and silverware. But, first, he turned to Zoey. "Could you go see about Charlie? It's time to eat, and he's still playing around in the bathwater. He has a bug to show you."

Zoey nodded, grinning. "He's going to be an excellent entomologist." She headed for the bathroom.

"What the hell is an entomologist?" Frida grinned.

"Someone who studies bugs," Logan replied.

"Oh, how exciting." Frida made a face.

Cass found himself taking a long look at Dylan. He was very curious about her. Okay, yeah. She's a looker, he said to himself. Her long, auburn hair was lovely, and she was very pretty. She was quiet, and didn't rattle on like some of the others. He liked that about her, too. But mostly, he wondered how someone could go from being a professional tattoo artist to a certified public accountant. He wanted to know more about her.

Zoey managed to get Charlie out of the bath, dried off, dressed, and at the table in record time. When they joined everyone, Zoey said to Logan in a low voice, "Pinacate beetle. That's what Charlie found. A pinacate beetle."

Logan chuckled. "Good to know." He poured wine for everyone, and juice for Charlie.

Li stood and said, "I'm making the toast tonight. To Frida!" He raised his wineglass. "What we all love about Frida is her energy, her optimism, and her persistence. All those corporate types who resist unionization and better working conditions for their employees better watch out and stay on Frida's good side, or they will be sorry!"

"Hear. Hear. To Frida!" were the words heard around the table.

"Want to say anything, Frida?" Logan asked.

Frida stood and grinned at everyone. "Thank you for this potluck. Thank you for your love and support. You are the best family I've ever had." She turned to Li. "And thank you, Li, for finding my kitty Bonita when she got out the other day. A coyote could have eaten her in one big bite. So thank you so much!"

"Can I play with Bonita again?" Charlie asked.

"Of course. Maybe you could stay with me for a while and play with Bonita when your daddy goes on a date." Frida looked at Logan and grinned, then noticeably shifted her gaze to Zoey. Logan turned pink, and Zoey looked down at her hands. Those two had a reputation among the Casa Pacifica friends for being in the early stages of a romance, but both seemed too shy to move forward. Frida was doing her best to help them get over themselves and take the next step.

"So let's eat!" Frida declared.

After stuffing themselves and, at the same time, chatting constantly, Logan began to collect the dishes. Dylan and Zoey helped him to move everything back into the kitchen. Zoey handed small plates to Charlie, and he distributed them to every place at the table.

Logan brought the cake out and lit the candles. "Make a wish, Frida, and blow out your candles."

Frida pressed her hand against her heart and closed her eyes. When she opened them again, she bent forward and blew out all the candles. Everyone cheered and sang "Happy Birthday" to her.

Li laughed. "You can bet Frida's wish has to do with that new contract she's negotiating with the grocery store chain."

Frida grinned. "I'm not saying anything. I want my wish to come true."

After an hour of amiable conversation, Charlie said goodnight, and, with Logan's help, he went to bed. When Logan returned, Cass stood and smiled at everyone. "Happy Birthday, Frida. It's time for me to say goodnight. I just finished a job, and I'm taking a little time off so I'll see you around."

After he'd closed the door behind him, Li and Frida both asked Logan at the same time, "What's his job?"

Logan hesitated. "Cass is in law enforcement. If you want details, you can ask him. The job he just finished had to do with taking down some drug dealers."

Everyone nodded approvingly.

"I'm next," Dylan said. She stood and waved to Frida. "Happy Birthday, girlfriend. And many more."

Frida whispered to Dylan before she could get away. "Are you going to go check out Cass?"

"Yep. And I'm not shy."

"I know you're not. I like the idea of another romance developing in Casa Pacifica. Cass is a hottie." Frida grinned.

"I'm just curious about him. That's all." Dylan smiled. "I'm going to fetch a sweater. It's chilly this evening. Happy Birthday again, Frida."

Sunset had come already, and the evening sky was dusky. Dylan found Cass sitting out in the side yard. She approached him.

"Okay to sit with you for a little while?" Dylan asked. "This is my favorite time of day."

He turned toward her and smiled. "Sure. Have a seat."

They sat in easy silence for a few minutes.

Cass turned toward her and said, "You want to know something, don't you?"

Dylan chuckled. "Yes, I do. I'd like to get to know you a little better."

"Good. Same here. I'd like to know you better." Cass was both curious and pleased.

More silence. Finally Dylan said, "Okay, I'll start. I'm an animal lover."

"I am, too."

"My favorites are horses and dogs."

He turned toward her, surprised. "Me, too. Dogs I get, but why horses?"

"I grew up on a horse farm in Kentucky. I've always lived around horses. They are lovely creatures. So full of heart. So loving."

Cass nodded. "I grew up on a horse farm like you."

"You did?" Dylan was genuinely surprised.

"Yes, I grew up near a little town called Whiteriver on the Fort Apache Reservation north of here. My people are Western Apache, White Mountain tribe."

"So you know all about horses?"

Cass nodded. "I do. I'd rather spend time with a horse than with most people."

"I can agree with that," Dylan said. "I have a horse now. I board her at a stable on the far east side of Tucson, and

I go out on the weekends for rides. She's an old girl now so we go easy on the rides. Her name is Betty."

"Betty?" Cass chuckled.

"I was a kid when she and I bonded. I thought that name was perfect for her back then. When I moved out here, she came with me."

"That must have been a big deal, bringing a horse with you all the way from Kentucky."

Dylan shrugged her shoulders. "She's been a lot of trouble and a big expense. But she's my best friend, and I want to make sure she has a good life until the end."

More quiet.

"Okay. So you know all about me. Tell me something about you." Dylan looked at him.

"Well, I don't really know *all* about you. I'd like to know more. But I get what you're saying. So what would you like to know about me?" Cass smiled.

"When you left the potluck, Frida and Li asked Logan what kind of work you do. He said law enforcement, and we're supposed to ask you if we want to know more."

"Sure you want to know?"

Dylan nodded. "I want to know."

"I'm an FBI Special Agent."

"Interesting. So how did you get from a kid on a horse farm on the reservation to being an FBI Special Agent."

Cass shook his head and chuckled. "I don't usually talk about this, but I guess I'll tell you since you're interested. Here goes. Right after I graduated from high school, I joined the U.S. Army. You know? See the world. Have an adventure. I did a tour in Afghanistan."

"See the world. Have an adventure. And get shot at?"

"Yeah. In my case, it wasn't shot *at*. It was just plain old shot. I was wounded pretty badly and sent home. I ended up back on the rez at my parents' place so I could recuperate fully."

"Then what happened?"

"You're good at interrogation, you know?" He grinned.

Dylan chuckled. "Thank you. That's a compliment coming from a Special Agent."

Cass chuckled. "Okay. So I got better. I worked at my parents' place and enrolled in the local community college. When I finished there, I moved to Flagstaff and finished a bachelor's degree at Northern Arizona University. The GI Bill paid for my education. Then I joined the Shadow Wolves. After a few years there, and getting shot again, this time by smugglers, I joined the FBI."

"Oh, my god! You were a Shadow Wolf! They are so amazing! I read that they are a special Homeland Security unit, all Native Americans, and they are brilliant trackers. They can find everything and everybody in the desert."

"We're pretty good at tracking, but I wouldn't say we can find *everything* and *everybody*."

"I'm impressed. So you got shot again and decided to move to the FBI where life would be easier?" She laughed and shook her head.

"Something like that." Cass found Dylan's questions very amusing.

"Have you been shot while in the FBI?"

"Not yet." He grinned. "Enough about me. Your turn. Tell me why you moved from Kentucky to Arizona, and why you went from tattoo artist to accountant."

"I'll condense this down. Because they were aging, my parents decided to give up the horse farm and stables. They passed it onto my brother, and they moved into town. He's supposed to pay me a share of the farm's earnings on a regular basis as my part of the inheritance. But he has a wife and four kids, and it costs a lot to run the place. So I never see much coming from him. I had to find a way of making a living."

"Why a tattoo artist?"

"I made a big mistake. It's a long story."

Cass nodded. "Okay. Save it for later."

"I have more questions for you."

"Shoot."

"I don't want to shoot you." She grinned.

He shook his head and chuckled. "Okay. Ask me another question."

"How tall are you?"

"Six three."

"Are you married or do you have a girlfriend?"

He grinned. "Nope."

"Last question. Would you like to go horseback riding with me sometime?"

"I would like that very much." He was surprised at how pleased he felt in that moment.

Dylan stood up. "Okay. I'm going in now."

"Yes. You're a very good interrogator." Cass could hear her laughing as she walked away.

2. Shot Again

Morning. Cass Cosay was up early again, just as he had been every day this week. He loved early morning, especially those precious moments just before the sun appeared over the Rincon Mountains in the eastern sky when everything was waking up. Or going to bed. He saw a couple of coyotes across the street trotting by, focused on their goal. They looked like they were headed to their resting place for the day. Hunt at night. Sleep during the day. The song dog's life.

He liked the evenings, especially when lovely young women interrogated him about his life. He laughed softly at the memory of Dylan Scott approaching him on Sunday after the potluck dinner. And she wasn't shy about asking questions. Much to his surprise, he'd been willing to answer. He didn't usually share much about his life. And what she told him about herself was very interesting. He wondered if she'd ever visited the Fort Apache reservation. He was quite certain that she would really enjoy horseback riding on the reservation's many trails.

After a quick cup of coffee, he put on some cut off blue jeans and an old t-shirt and went jogging. He enjoyed a trip around the Iron Horse neighborhood on his run. Most of the houses were older and on small lots, and there was a small park and community garden on the southern border. He was discovering a few businesses, including a small grocery market, that were scattered throughout the neighborhood. The Iron Horse neighborhood was just east of very busy Fourth Avenue, which provided Tucsonans and visitors easy access to restaurants, bars, night clubs, and businesses of all sorts, including drug dealers who regularly and surreptitiously sought potential buyers. At least some of them were out of business now that he and his team had taken them down about five days ago. Busted and in jail. That's where they belonged.

After the bust, Cass decided to take a couple of weeks off. He wanted to think about things. About his life. He'd been an FBI Special Agent for several years, and a Shadow Wolf before that. He was thinking maybe it was time for a change. Or not. He had a good career with the FBI. The work was interesting, if dangerous at times. But did he want to do it forever? He couldn't say. Sometimes he really missed the reservation. His dad had passed on now, but his mother and siblings all lived there. He missed the quiet of the rez and the beauty of the landscape. He missed the horses. That was something he and Dylan agreed about – the horses. Maybe it was time to go home for a visit.

Back at the apartment, Cass showered and ate a quick breakfast. He settled down in a comfortable chair in front of the big window facing the south. He had a good science-fiction book to read, and he could watch a film on the television, if he felt like it. Later, he'd take a long walk. But mainly, he just wanted to take time to think about his life and what he wanted next. Logan Reid, the apartment manager, came to mind. Cass was a little jealous of Logan because he was a father. Cass had always wanted a kid, or more than one, but he could see it was really challenging, especially because Logan was a single father. Charlie was an adorable handful. Nope, not easy. Cass figured he was better off finding a good woman to share those child-rearing duties. Was he ready for that? Ready for marriage and parenting? He wasn't sure.

And where exactly does one find a "good woman?" He had only been in love, really in love, once in his life. She was a fellow soldier, but she was discharged a few months before him, and she went home. They drifted apart because it was just too difficult to maintain a long distance relationship over several months and from opposite sides of the world. The last time he heard from her, she was marrying some other man. Since then, his interactions with women mostly had not been all that satisfying. Nothing serious. It was that way for the women as well. Just fun and some physical, meaning sexual, affection. Not real love. He hadn't found the right woman. Cass sighed and opened his book.

The day went by slowly. Cass called his mom and had a nice conversation with her. He took a nap. He baked some bread. He read some more. He watched the news on the television. He realized that it was a little after five, and because of that, there was a chance that he might see Dylan returning home. He liked seeing the sun on her dark red hair. "Auburn" was the term. The accounting firm where she worked was on Fourth Avenue not far away, and several times, he'd seen her returning home on foot in the late afternoon. He thought if he saw her today maybe he could ask her when she wanted to go riding.

Yes, there she was. Dylan was moving at a steady pace along the sidewalk and coming closer and closer to Casa Pacifica. She was dressed in a dark blue business suit, and she was carrying her dress shoes in her hand. She had canvas shoes on her feet, a purse was hanging from her shoulder, and her hair was pinned up. Very attractive woman. Cass stood up.

Suddenly a small car pulled up to the curb and stopped right next to Dylan. Three young men got out. They looked to be maybe early or mid-twenties. Dylan had stopped, but not for long. When she attempted to walk quickly away, one of the young men reached out and grabbed her. Or, more accurately, he grabbed one of her breasts really roughly. Cass was on his feet now, headed for the door. By the time he got down the stairs, he could see through the glass that the other two men had trapped Dylan between them. They were lifting her up off her feet, and the one who had grabbed her breasts was now running his hand up her skirt. All three of them were laughing and carrying her toward their car.

Cass knew exactly what they were up to. They were going to abduct her, take her some place quiet and out of the way, and each of them would have a go at her in the backseat of their car. Then they would dump her out on the street and drive away. Bastards. By the time he shoved open the downstairs door and ran toward them, one of them had torn open her blouse and was trying to pull away her bra to expose her breasts. Dylan was kicking and struggling, and when she attempted to scream, one of them punched her face.

"Hey!" Cass yelled. "Let her go!"

The three young men froze for a moment, staring at Cass. One of them looked intently at him and growled. "We know you, *pendejo*. You took down our amigos last week and ruined our sales. We lost a lot of money because of you." He pulled a small pistol from his belt and pointed it at Cass.

"No!" Dylan cried out. She struggled against the men who held her, and she violently thrust her body into one of them who then fell against the guy with the pistol. When the gun went off, the bullet missed Cass's chest and went instead into his leg just above his knee.

The two men holding Dylan dropped her, and the three of them jumped into their car and sped away, tires screaming.

Cass limped rapidly toward Dylan who was on the sidewalk now.

"Got your cell phone?" he asked.

"My cell phone?"

"Yeah. I want to record their license plate number."

Dylan was giggling now as she handed him her cell phone. "Oh, I thought you were going to get my number so you could ask me out on a date." The giggles changed into sobs.

Cass recorded the license number in the notepad on her phone.

"I'll ask you out later," he grinned. "Are you okay?"

"Just beat up a little. More relevant is, are *you* okay? You're bleeding." She wiped away the tears streaming down her face.

Cass looked down at his leg. Yep. Blood was staining his jeans just above the knee.

"Okay to use your phone to call the cops?"

"Sure." Dylan struggled to stop the tears. She found some tissues in her purse.

Cass made quick calls to the Sheriff's Department, to Border Patrol, and to the local FBI office. His message was a quick description of the assault on Dylan, what the young man said to him about the bust on Fourth Avenue, and the Sonora, Mexico, license plate number. His last words to all three were, "They'll most likely head for the border. Try to catch them before they cross over, and don't forget that one of them has a gun."

Cass turned and walked a few steps away from Dylan. She was struggling with her clothing, attempting to cover her bra and button up her torn blouse. Cass called the

Tucson Police Department and asked for Detective Alvarez. He explained the situation and asked Alvarez to come to them at Casa Pacifica.

"But give us an hour or so. I need to make sure Dylan is okay because she got roughed up pretty badly. Oh, yeah. And I got shot. It's not bad."

Alvarez protested, saying that he could call for an ambulance.

"No. Not that bad. Come in an hour." He disconnected.

Cass walked back to Dylan and returned the phone. He bent down to take a good look at her. "You're going to have a black eye, and I can see what he did. He grabbed you hard there." He pointed to her breasts. "And put his hand up your skirt. And tore your blouse. Come on. Let's go to your apartment. I want to make sure you're okay."

"Oh, you!" she giggled. The tears started to flow again. "You got shot, and you're worried about my torn clothes and a couple of bruises? I'm taking you to the emergency room."

"It's not that bad. I think it's just a flesh wound."

"No! Come with me. Let's go to my car. It's parked in the back." She stood up, straightened her spine, squared her shoulders, and stuck her chin out. She approached him and said, "Put your arm on my shoulders, and I'll help you walk to my car."

Cass shook his head, grinning. "Seriously. It's not that bad."

"Shut up." She glared at him.

He realized in that moment that Dylan was attempting to deal with the traumatic emotional impact of a violent assault on her body. If telling him what to do made her feel in control of her life again, he'd go along with that.

She pointed at his leg. "See! Still bleeding. We're going to get you some medical care."

Cass did as she said, trying to not laugh. Yeah, the wound hurt a little, but he knew what a serious gunshot wound felt like. This wasn't that serious. Probably the bullet just grazed him. He was almost certain it hadn't entered his leg. He was bleeding but not that much.

"You're kinda pushy, you know?" He couldn't help himself. He chuckled.

Dylan looked up at him. "You just now figuring that out?" She had tears in her eyes, but he could see the beginnings of a smile. "Seriously, Cass. You should follow my instructions. Your life will be so much better if you do what I say."

"Yes, ma'am." He couldn't stop the chuckles. "But I think the emergency room is too much."

"Okay, Mr. Stubborn. Will you settle for a trip to one of those walk-in urgent care centers? There's one not far from here."

"If that makes you happy." He couldn't stop grinning.

"Yes, that makes me happy. And you definitely want to make me happy."

Much to his great surprise, he realized that this is exactly what he wanted. He wanted Dylan Scott to be happy, and he wanted to be the man who made her happy.

"Will you let them look at you, too?" he asked.

"Not necessary."

"Bullshit. Who's the stubborn one? Do me a favor. Let's both get looked at by the medics. Please."

By now, they had half-walked, half-limped to the small parking lot behind the Casa Pacifica apartments. Cass removed his arm from her shoulders, and Dylan opened the passenger door. She gestured for him to get in.

"You didn't answer me." He looked directly at her.

"Okay! I'll get seen by a medic. Now get in the car and be good."

21

He was laughing as he carefully placed himself in the car seat and closed the door. Be good? The last time someone told him to be good, he was probably seven or eight years old. He tried to stifle the laughter. The wound wasn't bleeding anymore, but it definitely hurt.

Dylan got in behind the wheel, and reached over and fastened his seat belt. She looked at him. "What the hell is wrong with you? You Indian warriors are supposed to be all stoic and serious all the time. But you can't stopped laughing."

"That's a stereotype. We Native Americans," he grinned, "we like to have fun as much as everybody else. And I'm not a warrior. I'm an FBI Special Agent."

"Same thing. And you've been shot, and you can't stop laughing."

"You'll have to admit. You're pretty funny."

"I am not."

Dylan pulled out of the parking place and headed for the street.

"Let me guess." Cass grinned. "When you were growing up, you took care of a little brother a lot."

"And four of my cousins. Five little boys. Pains in the butt, every single one."

"That's what made you such a tyrant, then." He pressed his lips together so he wouldn't laugh again.

Dylan looked at him. "Lucky you. I'm going to take care of you, like it or not. And stop laughing. This isn't funny."

"I think I detect a smile on your beautiful face. You think this is a little bit funny, don't you? Admit it."

"Maybe just a teeny, tiny, little bit funny. Now be quiet. We'll be at the urgent care place in a few minutes." She was smiling now. "Who knew you are such a gigglepuss?"

"A gigglepuss? Oh, my god." Cass laughed again. "What the hell is that?"

She glanced over at him. "I guess you don't want your FBI colleagues to know your true nature, do you, Mr. Gigglepuss?"

Cass looked down and shook his head. "I could never live that down."

"Then you better do what I say."

"Oh, my god. Coercion. Threats. Arm twisting. I'm under severe duress." He laughed again.

Dylan shook her head. "Here we are." She pulled off the street and into the urgent care parking lot.

They went into the center, and checked in with the receptionist. Within minutes, Cass's name was called.

Dylan stood up. "Come on." She pulled him up by his arm.

"You go first," he said.

"Shut up." She took his hand and pulled him into the exam room.

"What can I do for you?" the medic asked.

Cass could see the medic's name tag. Mary Something. She was a nurse practitioner.

"This is Cass Cosay," Dylan said. "He was shot when he rescued me from three gangsters who tried to abduct and rape me."

"Good grief." Mary Something looked at Cass, then down at his leg. "You were shot there just above your knee?"

"That's right. I don't think it's serious."

"Okay. Let's see," said the nurse.

Cass inserted himself between Dylan and the nurse with his back to Dylan. He unzipped his blue jeans and lowered them.

"Going commando, huh?" the nurse said.

Cass could hear Dylan giggling. He was embarrassed.

"He's giving me a treat, a very nice view of a very nice butt." Dylan laughed.

"I haven't had a chance to go to the laundromat lately."

"You don't have to. There's a little laundry downstairs in our apartment building. I'll show you."

"Sit here." The nurse pointed to an examination table. "I'll give you a paper gown to cover yourself." Cass followed her directions. The nurse took a good look at the wound. "I think you're right. It's a flesh wound. The bullet tore a chunk of skin and some muscle, but it didn't go into your leg so didn't hit an artery or a major vein or the bone."

Cass nodded. That's what he thought. Not serious.

"I'll disinfect the wound, bandage it, and give you a pain killer prescription. You don't even need any stitches. You got lucky. I'll just tape this up."

"Okay." The sooner he got out of there, the better. Cass had many unhappy memories of far more serious wounds. This was nothing.

Five minutes of silence followed as the nurse did her work. She stood. "You can stand up and pull up your jeans now."

"Aw, does he have to?" Dylan giggled. The nurse also laughed.

Cass looked at her, then back at the nurse. He rolled his eyes and sighed heavily. "What about her? She got hurt, too."

"Okay, trade places." Dylan came forward and Cass sat down in a chair against the wall.

The nurse took a good look at Dylan's face, paying special attention to the area around her eye. She had Dylan follow a small light with her eyes.

"Looks like you were hit on this bone just under your eye, but the eye appears to be okay. You'll have a big bruise where that guy hit you."

Dylan nodded. "I can live with that."

"Did he hit you anywhere else?"

"No, but he grabbed my breast really hard. It hurts."

"Let's take a look," the nurse said.

"Can I see, too?" Cass grinned.

Dylan turned toward him and said, "Mind your own business."

"Yes, ma'am." He chuckled.

She pulled away her torn blouse.

"Hmm. I already see bruises forming. Bruises in the shape of fingers."

Cass had this sudden wave of anger come over him. Too bad those little shits had ran off so fast. He would have been quite pleased to show them a thing or two.

"That's okay, then," Dylan said. "So I'll have bruises and a black eye. I'll get over that pretty fast."

"I don't think you need any meds. Just give yourself some time. And don't let anymore guys grab you."

"Unless I want to be grabbed." Dylan laughed. She glanced over her shoulder at Cass.

"Oh, my god," Cass groaned. "You're a piece of work. I thought you were so quiet and shy."

"Yeah, that's me. Quiet and shy." She turned to the nurse. "Thanks very much."

They returned to the reception area and Dylan paid for their care.

"You should let me pay," Cass said.

"Hush. Think about what you want to eat for supper."

On their way back to Casa Pacifica, they went through a fast food drive-through restaurant, and they ordered veggie burgers, fries, and juice drinks.

"I've never had a veggie burger," Cass said.

"You'll like it."

He chuckled. "Yes, ma'am. If you say so." They went to Cass's apartment.

25

"You're limping," she said, as they climbed the stairs.

"Yeah. I'll get over it."

Dylan's phone rang. "One moment, please." She handed the phone to Cass.

He took it and said hello. "Hello. Oh, yeah. Officer Alvarez. Thanks for calling. Want to come by? We'll let you know what happened."

Alvarez showed up about twenty minutes later. Cass and Dylan had just finished eating.

"You seem to be running into a lot of bad guys, Agent Cosay," Alvarez said, smiling. He and Cass had met earlier when Cass took down a shooter who was threatening Nina Perry and her jazz band members.

Cass shrugged his shoulders and smiled. He spent a few minutes telling Alvarez about what had happened, the attempted abduction and getting shot in the leg. Then it was Dylan's turn.

"I already reported this to Border Patrol and to my FBI supervisor," Cass explained. "We should know by tomorrow if these guys made a run for the border, and if they were caught."

Alvarez flipped his notebook closed. "Okay. I'm glad the gunshot wound isn't bad. And Miss Scott, I'm glad you are okay."

Dylan smiled and gestured to Cass. "He rescued me."

Alvarez nodded. "We'll let you know if we learn more. And let's hope Border Patrol or the Sheriff deputies catch those troublemakers. I'll be in touch." Alvarez stood and said goodbye.

When he was gone, Dylan looked directly at Cass and said, "I'm going back to my apartment. I have some work to do this evening for one of my accounts. But I want to say…" She reached out and took his hand. "I want to say thank you for rescuing me. I'm pretty sure they were going to kidnap and rape me. All three of them. You saved me from a terrible trauma. And you rescued me. And you made me laugh. Thank you, Mr. Cass Cosay, Apache warrior and FBI Special Agent." She smiled.

Cass returned her smile. "The next time I get shot, I want to get shot with you. You're lots of fun."

Dylan stood, leaned forward and kissed him on the cheek. "I'll show you the laundry tomorrow." She went to the door to leave.

As she opened the door, Cass heard her say softly, "Mr. Gigglepuss." He stood and limped quickly to Dylan, put his hands on her shoulders and said, "Every time you say that word, I'm going to shut you up."

"You mean the word 'gigglepuss'?"

"Shut up." Cass leaned down and kissed her firmly on her lips. He turned her around and nudged her into the hallway. "Now scoot," he said, and he closed the door behind her. He could hear Dylan laughing as she walked away.

3. A Watchful Eye

The next morning, Cass called Border Patrol and his FBI supervisor. The Border Patrol agent had good news about the three men who attempted to assault Dylan.

"Yep, we got 'em. They went zipping by our post 42 just north of Tubac. They were driving way too fast on Highway I-19 heading south for the border. Two Santa Cruz County Sheriff's deputies were there at our post, and when they saw the speeders, they cut across the highway and went after them. The deputies had already received a call from their department to watch for these three, and thanks to you, we had their Sonora license plate number. We have them in custody now."

"Excellent work," Cass said. "You'll be hearing more from Pima County Sheriff or the Tucson Police Department because of an assault and attempted rape they committed here in Tucson. And one of them shot me."

"Oh, jeez," the Border Patrol agent said. "Are you both okay?"

"Yeah, just a flesh wound. The woman is roughed up, but she's okay, too. I'm looking forward to seeing these dudes hauled off for a lengthy stay in prison. Thanks again."

Next, Cass called his supervisor at the FBI field office in Phoenix, Agent Dexter. Cass went over the events of the day before.

"You know about the busts we did about five days ago," Cass began. "The fact that one of these dudes referenced the bust is really bugging me. He seemed to have recognized me immediately."

"So you think the woman who was attacked might have been just a ruse to get you out on the street so they could take you down?"

"I just don't know. It's clear that they weren't just playing around with the woman. They were in the process of abducting her, and I'm sure all three would have raped her. But if they already knew that I was in the nearby apartment, and if they knew I had been keeping an eye out, it would have been a sure-fire way to lure me out. Eliminating me with a well-aimed bullet would not only stop me from going after their gang again, it would be an act of revenge that would raise their reputation among the drug dealers."

Dexter was quiet for a few seconds, then he said, "I suggest you ask around and see if any neighbors saw those three scoping out your part of town. If they had been seen earlier, then it is definitely possible that they knew where you live, and they were trying to get to you. If not, it could simply be that they saw a vulnerable woman and decided to have their sick idea of fun with her. It's possible that she was the target all along. It could have been a spontaneous act with no connection to you."

"Yes. That's why I'm not sure. I'm going to ask my apartment manager if he's seen them or anyone else suspicious. He's often around and keeps an eye on things."

"Watch your back, Cosay. You might consider lying low for a while and not attracting any attention."

"Definitely. Thanks for the input. Talk to you later."

Cass drank another cup of coffee. Time to go see Logan. He headed downstairs, noticing right away that the wound on his leg was better. The limp was almost gone, and the pain was far less. He knocked on Logan's door. "Are you home, Logan?"

Logan answered. "Yeah. Come on in, Cass."

"Are you busy?"

"Well, sort of. This is spring break at the university, and my students just turned in their homework essays before the break began. I'm reading and grading their papers now. But I could use a break. Have a seat."

They went into Logan's living room area in front of the big window that looked out on the street. They sat in stuffed chairs.

"Where's Mr. Motor Mouth?" Cass had heard Logan refer to his son that way.

Logan chuckled. "Mr. Motor Mouth is with Ms. Biology Teacher again. They hunted for bugs first, then next came the reptiles."

"Reptiles? Yikes!" Cass laughed.

"Yeah, I was worried about that, too. Zoey showed him videos of rattlesnakes and with a sound track so he could hear the rattling. She followed up with appropriate warnings. Then they went looking for lizards, including a horned lizard, known as a horny toad."

"Can't beat those horny toads. They eat ants. My sibs and I used to catch them when we were kids. We turned them over in our hands and rubbed their bellies. They always fell asleep."

Logan grinned. "Today Charlie and Zoey are bird watching. Zoey has some app on her phone that identifies their songs so Charlie and Zoey can id the birds even if they can't see them. Zoey told me that birds would be the focus of most of their time."

"She's taking a lot of interest in Charlie."

Logan nodded. "They get along great, and Charlie loves every minute with her."

"Ah, a little scientist in the making."

"Right." Logan was quiet for a moment. He knew Zoey and Charlie had made a connection when she shared with him that her son had died from a severe illness when he was only three. Logan thought that spending time with Charlie might be a way for Zoey to deal with her grief at the loss of her child.

Cass said, "I've been thinking I'd like to be a dad, but I don't know if I can do it. And I have to find the right woman."

"You can do it. The love for your kid is so intense that you'll figure it out as you go along." Logan paused. "About the woman, you probably heard about my wife who died of a brain aneurysm when Charlie was two years old."

"Nina told me. She told me all about everyone in Casa Pacifica."

Logan nodded. "I've been thinking it might be time for me to start seeing women again."

"That makes sense. It's been three years, right?"

Logan nodded. "Three and a half."

"Zoey looks like a good option. She's not attached to anyone, she and Charlie enjoy each other, she likes you, you like her. Only one problem."

"What?" Logan had a worried look on his face.

"You take her to bed, have really hot sex with her, and then the next morning, you find a lizard in your bed."

Logan laughed.

"I say go for it." Cass grinned.

"Okay. I'll ask Zoey out for a date. Enough about me. What's on your mind?" Logan asked.

"I have a story to tell you." Cass was serious now. He recounted the assault on Dylan, how he got shot in the leg, and their trip to get medical care. He described in detail the three men and their car.

"Good god, man. Are you okay? And Dylan. I haven't seen her since the Sunday pot luck. Is she okay?"

"Yeah, we're both fine. Actually it turned out to be kind of a laugh. She's really a lot of fun, a real tyrant who likes to push me around. Very amusing. I laughed a lot." Cass paused, smiling. "Anyway, Sheriff deputies caught the perps who were heading for the border. They are in custody now in Santa Cruz County. I'm here to ask you if you had seen these guys or their car in our neighborhood recently."

He held out his phone to Logan. "They sent me arrest mugshots of these three this morning. Recognize any of them?"

Logan looked closely at the photos. "No. I haven't seen any of them. Will you email me these photos? They might not stay in jail. And they might have some friends around here."

"Sure. There's an outside chance that these guys were here to bring me down since I busted some of their druggie business associates recently. And Dylan was just an opportunity for a little nasty fun that they couldn't pass up."

Logan shook his head and frowned.

"She invited me to go horseback riding on Saturday." Cass smiled.

"Nice. I bet you know how to ride a horse."

Cass chuckled. "Yeah. I grew up with horses on the rez."

"Hey, that might be something fun to do with Zoey and Charlie," Logan said. "Maybe a little pony for Charlie."

"If not a pony, try an older, very calm mare. They are usually good with kids."

"Good idea. I'll talk to Zoey about that."

Cass stood up. "Time for me to go. Thanks for the conversation, Logan. You're an okay dude, you know. Yeah, I say go for it. Zoey, I mean. Not horses or lizards."

Logan grinned. "I must admit that idea of hot sex is very compelling, with or without a lizard."

* * *

After Cass left, Logan gave up on grading papers for a while. He sat on his sofa and thought about recent events.

First, what Cass had told him was very worrisome. It was bad enough that anyone would be assaulted in his neighborhood. But that the assault happened to one of his tenants, a Casa Pacifica resident, was simply unacceptable. If anything like this happened again, he was going to ask for Tucson police to start driving by on a regular basis to intimidate anyone thinking of perpetrating this kind of crime. He also would bring this up at the Sunday potluck and warn everyone to be paying attention. And Cass getting shot. That was awful. He was so grateful that Cass had not been seriously wounded. Logan liked him and wanted the best for Cass, especially since he fit in so well with the other Casa Pacifica residents.

Of even greater concern, though, was Charlie's safety. Charlie often played out in the yard. Logan wanted to make sure he was always under the watchful eye of an adult, and that he would always be safe.

A watchful eye? Other than himself, he figured that there was no one better than Zoey Corban to be keeping watch over him. And she was teaching his son all that science stuff and having fun at the same time. Charlie always came home happy after he'd been with Zoey.

Logan sighed. You're an idiot, he said to himself. What have you been waiting for? He had to face the fact that he'd avoided thinking about Zoey, or more accurately, Zoey as a woman, not Zoey as someone to spend time with his five-year-old son. True. He couldn't think of anything in his life more traumatic than Caroline's sudden death. He had been overwhelmed with grief. He buried himself in his work at the university, in taking care of Charlie, and in taking care of everyone but himself.

Time had come now to think about himself. Zoey. Sweet, funny, kindhearted Zoey. Zoey who loved Charlie. Zoey who was loved by Charlie. Zoey, pretty, nice curves, very touchable. Okay. Admit it, you fool. She's sexy. Logan felt a thrill go up his spine. Zoey. Hot sex with Zoey. Oh, god.

Start easy, he warned himself. Ask her out with Charlie along. The three of them. Then not long after, ask her on a real date. Just the two of them. A real date. Just Zoey and himself. Yeah, ease into it.

As if on cue, he heard a noise in the hall. Then Charlie's voice. "I'm going to go see Daddy." Three seconds later, his boy burst through the apartment door.

"Daddy! I'm home. Zoey and I went bird watching."

Zoey entered the apartment, grinning from ear to ear.

"Watch this, Logan." She pulled her phone out. "Charlie, please identify these bird calls for your dad."

Charlie nodded, grinning and wiggling in excitement.

She clicked on the phone. Logan could hear a raucous call.

"Gila woodpecker." Charlie giggled.

"Correct," Zoey said. "This one?" Another bird sang.

"Lesser goldfinch."

"Correct." Logan recognized the next one.

"Dove. Mourning dove," Charlie said.

"Correct."

"I hear that one a lot," Logan said.

"Last one," Zoey said. She held up the phone. Another bird song.

"Phainopepla." Charlie stumbled a bit over the word. "Daddy, that one looks like a cardinal but it's black. It's not red. It's black. We saw it."

"Really? I didn't know that." He gave Charlie a hug. "Well done, son. I'm impressed." He kissed Charlie on his forehead. He looked up at Zoey and smiled. "Thank you, Zoey."

"Charlie probably needs something to eat." She smiled at Logan.

"Okay. It's lunch time. Then he can take a nap."

"Guess I'll go," Zoey said. "Thanks, Charlie."

"Stay and eat lunch with us," Logan said. "I can make some grilled cheese sandwiches. And cut up some avocados."

"Sure. I'll help you."

Lunch came together pretty fast. While they ate, Logan listened to Charlie tell him all about the hike they took and all the birds they'd identified, either by sight or sound.

They finished lunch. Logan looked at Zoey and said, "Charlie and I have been talking about going to a basketball game at McKale Center on the University of Arizona campus. The men's team is out of town now, but the women will be playing Saturday. Would you like to go with us?"

He couldn't help but notice that very pleased look that came over Zoey's face.

"Yes! Go with Daddy and me!" Charlie said.

"I would like that very much. Yes, I'll go with you to the basketball game."

"Good." Logan nodded. "Okay. Charlie, time for a nap."

Charlie hugged Logan and then went around the table to hug Zoey. He went off to his bedroom making bird sounds.

Logan sat down again. "Zoey?"

"Yes?"

"I...uh...well...uh...yeah...uh. I've been wondering."

"Yes?" She was smiling at him. She was so pretty. He felt himself getting warm.

"I'd like to ask you out. I mean, not you and me and Charlie. But just you and me. Like a date. I've been thinking about that. Just you and me. A date."

"Sure!" Zoey grinned. "Thank you, Logan. I would love to go out with you on a date."

Logan was surprised at how relieved he felt. Total relief. And he was surprised and pleased at how happy she looked to get his invitation.

"Okay. We'll look for a time that works for both of us. I have to arrange for Charlie to have some place safe to be. He's not going to Javie's house anytime soon because Javie and his family will be out of town."

"I have a student who could take care of Charlie for us."

"You do?" Logan noticed the phrase "for us," not "for you." "For us."

"She's a senior, very responsible and trustworthy. She wants to be an elementary school teacher, and she loves little kids. She'll be entering the university in the fall. Her name is Katie."

"She sound perfect."

"Could she bring her dog? The dog is a rescue, a good dog who will be fun for Charlie."

"Charlie would love that."

"Okay. So you choose a time for our date, and I'll arrange Katie to babysit for us."

There it was again. "For us." Logan was very pleased. "Excellent. I'll take a look at the schedule, and we'll arrange a time for our first date." And he hoped many more.

Zoey stood. "I'm going back to my apartment now. Let me know when to meet you to go to the basketball game."

Logan nodded. "Sure. And thanks for doing all that birding stuff with Charlie. He's learning so much from you, and he's having fun."

"Charlie is a lot of fun for me, too." She turned and went to the door. "See ya, Logan."

Logan sat in his chair and took a deep breath. Now that wasn't so hard, was it?

After a few minutes, Logan went to check on Charlie. Sound asleep. Then he made himself a cup of coffee and went back to grading essays. That didn't last long. He couldn't get his conversation with Cass out of his head. His neighborhood has always been relatively safe, even considering that it was part of a large city with a metro area of nearly one million people. He felt responsible both for Charlie and also for the residents in the Casa Pacifica apartments.

He retrieved his laptop and began searching. To begin, he looked at websites that posted pictures of criminals, their associates, their crimes and the criminal organizations they belonged to. He didn't find any photos of the three young men that Cass had sent him. Maybe the three who had attacked Dylan and shot Cass were young enough to be fairly new to the game, or maybe their photos just hadn't been posted yet.

Logan thought again about the young man who had targeted Nina Perry and her jazz group a couple of months earlier. That man had been hanging around watching the apartment building and even following Nina home from her gigs at the jazz club on Fourth Avenue. Visiting Canadian Gwilym Havard had been a great help in keeping Nina safe. Logan hadn't noticed the criminal until too late. He couldn't let that happen again. He wondered if maybe it was time to organize a neighborhood watch association. He sighed. Or not. Maybe he was overreacting. Cass seemed to think that the gang just saw an opportunity with Dylan, or alternatively, they were after Cass all along. Maybe the whole thing was an isolated event, and not part of a bigger movement toward more crime in his part of the city.

No matter. Logan vowed to himself to stay aware, to be on watch. He wanted his people to be safe.

4. HORSES AND BASKETBALL

Saturday morning came, and Dylan knocked on Cass's apartment door.

He opened it smiling. "I'm ready." He had on leather boots, jeans, a long-sleeve cotton shirt, and a western cowboy hat tilted back on his head.

Dylan grinned at him. "Ah, so Mr. Gigglepuss has transformed himself into a cowboy."

Cass's eyebrows went up. "I warned you not to call me that. So you can shut up now." He stepped forward and kissed her firmly.

"What a way to start the day." Dylan chuckled. "Now I know how to get a kiss from you."

He stepped back and looked at her. "You look like a real cowgirl. Jeans, long-sleeve shirt, boots, and that hat. The real thing."

"I am the real thing. Don't forget that, Mr. …"

He stepped toward her. She laughed. "Gotcha, smarty pants. You thought I was going to say 'gigglepuss.'" She hesitated. "Uh oh."

Cass laughed. He kissed her again.

She turned and headed down the stairs. "Enough of this fooling around. Let's go get in my car and drive to the stable."

At the bottom of the stairs, Dylan turned to Cass and said, "Looks like you're not limping much. Feeling better?"

"Yes, much better."

Half an hour later, they turned into a small acreage on the far east side of Tucson at the foot of the Rincon Mountains. The sign said, "Corazon Riding Stables and Boarding."

"Laurie used to be over in Cascabel. But there wasn't enough business there because it's so rural. So she moved closer to Tucson where there are more customers." Dylan pulled into a parking place. "Come on, and I'll introduce you."

At that moment, a woman, maybe in her mid-fifties, came out of a nearby barn. She was a little plump, not very tall, with a mass of blonde-gray curls on her head. She waved as she walked toward them. Dylan and Cass returned her wave.

"Hi, girlfriend. Come to see your Betty?"

"Yes. And I brought a friend. This is Cass Cosay. He thinks he maybe knows how to ride a horse."

Cass and Laurie exchanged handshakes.

"I'm Laurie James. Not experienced, huh? That's okay. We can find you an easy ride."

Cass glanced over at Dylan. She had pressed her lips together, trying her best to not laugh.

"Thank you, Miss James. I'm hoping I don't fall off the horse. Dylan will have to save me if I do."

Dylan couldn't help herself. She laughed out loud. "Sorry, Laurie. He knows how to ride. Cass used to be a Shadow Wolf."

Laurie's eyebrows went up in surprise. Then she grinned. "Okay. I've got a stallion for you that can be a bit feisty. We think he'll make a good stud so we're hoping to find him a girlfriend soon. Maybe that will calm him down. You could do us a favor. He really needs some exercise."

"I'll do my best to make friends with him. Yeah, a friendly mare will improve his attitude." Cass glanced over at Dylan. She had a wide grin on her face.

"I'll get Betty saddled and send her out. Then I'll bring out Tornado." Laurie turned and went back to the barn.

Cass grinned. "Okay. Tornado it is."

"Let's go this way, Cass," Dylan said. She took off walking toward a corral not far away. When they arrived, they both climbed up and sat at the top level. The corral was made of old-fashioned wood, not the more modern galvanized steel panels.

A teenage boy brought Betty out and led her to Dylan. The horse neighed her greeting to Dylan.

Cass looked closely at Dylan's horse. Betty was a mature chestnut mare with big brown eyes. She immediately approached Dylan who reached out and began stroking the horse's muzzle and cheeks. The horse pushed in closer and nuzzled Dylan. To Cass, it was clear that there was a lot of affection going both ways.

"She needs a little treat," Cass said. He reached into his pocket and pulled out a plastic bag full of baby carrots and a cut up apple. He offered one to Betty, and she took it politely. Crunch, crunch. The mare moved over and nuzzled Cass as he stroked her. She sighed. Satisfied.

"You're trying to seduce my horse," Dylan said.

"No, it's not Betty I'm trying to seduce." Cass didn't look at her. He just smiled. He heard Dylan chuckle. He gave Betty a piece of apple. More crunching. Another sigh.

"You're kind of a bad boy, aren't you?" Dylan said.

"No, I'm good." He looked directly at her. "*Very* good." He wiggled his eyebrows.

"Oh, goodness." She looked a little embarrassed.

Cass shook his head. "I'm not really a bad boy. After what happened, I just want to make you laugh."

Dylan's face fell. "Oh, yeah. I'm hoping to get past all that. Thank you, Cass. You do make me laugh. You're fun to be around."

"Here's an extra bag of treats for you and Betty." Cass handed the carrots and apples to Dylan.

At that moment, Laurie came out of the barn with a big, black stallion who was pulling on the lead, jerking his head, and moving quickly toward Betty. When Laurie pulled him back, Tornado pinned his ears back and kicked his hind legs. He neighed loudly in protest. Laurie anticipated this and had already moved out of the way.

Cass grinned. "Now there's your bad boy."

Laurie brought the horse to Cass who jumped down into the corral next to Tornado.

"Good luck, Cass. He really needs some exercise and some training," Laurie said.

Cass nodded. "I'll work with him."

Dylan reached out and gave a baby carrot to Betty, but before she could take it into her mouth, Tornado nipped her with his front teeth and grabbed the carrot.

Tornado jumped back in surprise when Cass thumped the horse's hock with toe of his boot.

"Give her another treat," Cass said to Dylan who complied. This time it was an apple slice.

When Tornado saw that, he began to move toward Betty again, but Cass pulled sharply on the lead and tapped the horse's hock again. Tornado neighed again.

"Come on, Tornado." Cass led him a few feet away. They walked around in a circle in the corral for a few minutes, then Cass led the horse back to where they'd been. After a few minutes, Cass began stroking Tornado's muzzle, and then he gave the stallion a chunk of apple. Crunch, crunch. Tornado shook his head up and down and moved in to nuzzle Cass. The horse got a carrot this time.

"Oh, I see what you're doing," Dylan said, "When Tornado tries to nip my horse, he gets that surprise tap on his hock, you pull him away, and he gets nothing. When he behaves, he gets a treat."

Cass nodded. "That's right. And I'll be consistent. If Tornado wants a treat, he has to forget about nipping Betty."

"I guess I could learn a thing or two from you," Dylan said. "The horses on my family's farm in Kentucky were mostly older and pretty well-behaved. I don't have any experience with a horse like Tornado."

Cass nodded. "I've been doing this since I was a kid. I've trained several horses, including some bad boys and a bad girl here and there." He looked at Dylan and smiled. "How about if we go for that ride you promised?"

* * *

At the same time that Cass and Dylan were heading off on their ride, Logan, Charlie, and Zoey joined a crowd of basketball lovers as they trekked to McHale Center on the University of Arizona campus. The three found their seats pretty quickly, and Charlie sat between Logan and Zoey.

"Does anyone want anything from the snack stand before the game starts?" Logan asked.

"I want some popcorn!" Charlie stood up and began moving up and down on his toes. "Can we have some popcorn? Please!"

"Sounds good to me. Maybe a bottle of water?" Zoey said.

Logan was gone for a few minutes and returned with a large bucket of popcorn and three bottles of water. The game began a few minutes later.

For Logan, the most fun thing about the next two hours was not the game itself, which was definitely fun, but how amusing it was to watch both Charlie and Zoey get into the game, clap and cheer, hoot and holler, and yell encouragement to the players or criticism to the referees. Zoey was definitely a sports fan, Logan decided. And Charlie. Absolutely a sports fan.

At one point, he asked Charlie, "Are you enjoying the game?"

"Hell, yeah!" Charlie giggled.

Zoey looked at Logan. She giggled, too.

Logan rolled his eyes. "See if you can find a better way to say that, Charlie."

The best moment for Logan, though, came when one of the Arizona Wildcat players threw the ball from way beyond the three-point arc only seconds before game ended. The Wildcats were down by one point so the shot meant the difference between losing or winning. The ball swooshed into the basket, the Wildcats got their three points, the crowd went wild, and the Cats won the game.

But it wasn't the victory that was so special. When the ball went in, Zoey squealed, then she reached over Charlie's head and threw her arms around Logan. She held him in a tight hug, and he could feel her warmth against him. He began pulling away to look at her, and that's when their cheeks came against each other, then their mouths and then their lips. He couldn't stop himself. He kissed her. And Zoey kissed him right back. She pulled away laughing. Yes, that was the best moment of the game.

After the game, they walked home to Casa Pacifica. Or more accurately, Logan and Zoey walked, and Charlie skipped. He talked the entire way home about how he was going to play basketball when he got big. And soccer. And baseball.

"I think you have a budding athlete on your hands, Logan." Zoey was smiling.

"Yes, no doubt in reaction to his nerdy, philosophy-loving dad."

"He may surprise you yet. He likes to learn things. But I think Charlie will more likely become a scientist, not a philosopher."

Logan grinned and took Zoey's hand. "That's your doing, Ms. Biology Teacher."

Charlie came running back to them. "I'm hungry!"

"Let's go home. We can make some supper."

"And watch a movie!" Charlie added. "Zoey, want to watch a movie with us?"

Logan looked at her and nodded. "We're going to watch *The Muppet Movie* for the second time. There's some dialog in it that is amusing for adults. It goes over Charlie's head, but I bet it will make you laugh. We'll enjoy watching it again and sharing with you."

"Okay, sounds like fun," Zoey said.

They made a quick meal in Logan's kitchen, ate, and cleaned up, then all three settled in on the sofa to watch the movie.

Halfway through the film, Logan realized that Charlie had fallen asleep. He turned to Zoey and said, "I have to go get him into his pajamas and into bed."

"Okay. I'm tired so I'm going home now. We can watch the movie another time." She stood, turned to him and said, "I love your son, Logan."

"Charlie loves you, Zoey."

"I hope someday Charlie's daddy will love me, too." Zoey went to his door. "Good night, Logan." Then she was gone.

Logan sat still, stunned at what she'd said.

* * *

Cass and Dylan took off at a lively trot down a wide, smooth trail leading away from the stables. Tornado tried to lead the way. The horse would have gone faster, but Cass held him to a reasonable pace. Cass was really enjoying himself. He couldn't stop grinning. Riding a horse in the wild Sonoran Desert, no cars, no computers, no sitting behind a desk, no one to arrest, no one shooting at him, no other people except the beautiful, auburn-haired woman on a horse beside him, all on a quiet, sunny March day. He couldn't ask for anything better. He kept glancing over at Dylan. She looked like she was born to be on a horse.

After about an hour, Dylan said, "Cass, see that grove of mesquite trees up ahead? Let's stop and rest a bit. I think Betty is getting tired." When they arrived at the grove, Dylan dismounted and led Betty to stand in the shade.

Cass did not dismount. "Dylan, this bad boy and I will be back in a few minutes." He turned away and squeezed his legs against Tornado. The quick trot turned into canter. Tornado threw his head back and pushed forward. It didn't take much pressure from Cass to get the horse into a full gallop. They flew down the hard-packed dirt road at almost full speed. Cass grabbed his cowboy hat so he wouldn't lose it. He couldn't stop grinning. Finally, he realized they were probably getting a little too far from Dylan and Betty. He slowed the horse back to a canter, and then a quick trot. They circled back to the mesquite grove. He could tell the horse was relaxed in a way that he hadn't been before. That's what Tornado needed, an all-out run on a regular basis. And Cass was the man to give him that. Cass knew he would be back to do this again. He would return to make sure that Tornado got a real run every week. And Cass. He needed this, too.

Cass and Tornado slowly trotted up to where Dylan and Betty were resting.

"You boys look like you've been taking a run. Did Tornado behave?"

"He's perfect. A perfect horse. He just needs to have his run on a regular basis." Cass gave Tornado a couple of apple and carrot treats. The horse crunched them and then nudged Cass playfully.

"Looks like you made a new friend."

"I'm coming back here again and take him for a run."

"Come and sit with me so Tornado can rest a bit before we head back."

Cass sat next to Dylan on a patch of dry grass.

"I've been wondering," Cass said. "Why did you ask me how tall I am when we talked the other evening? It's pretty obvious that I'm fairly tall." He smiled at Dylan.

"I was just wondering how long the stirrup straps attached to your saddle would need to be. Tall guys usually have long legs."

Cass nodded. "That makes sense. You knew you were going to invite me to go riding."

"Yes. That was the plan. And my plan worked." She grinned. "So tell me about you and horses."

"I told you already. I grew up with horses."

"What's the best thing you've ever done with a horse? Your best experience?" Dylan looked at him with a smile on her face.

Cass was quiet for a while. He nodded, and said, "Recapturing my native heritage with the horses."

"What do you mean?"

"Well, you know us Native Americans. There's lot of stereotypes about us, both positive and negative. But we're real people. So when we get around each other, we don't have to deal with all that stereotype stuff." He paused. "When I was a teenager, a couple of my Apache friends and I went to a pow wow in South Dakota, a Lakota pow wow on the Pine Ridge rez. We started hanging out with some boys from the Lakota tribe. They took us to a sanctuary for wild horses in the Black Hills not far from the rez. We all got rides for ourselves at a stable there, and we went out onto the prairie. Beautiful country. High grasslands prairie and the Rocky Mountains were on the horizon. We found a herd of wild horses. They took off so we followed. We caught up, and we ran with them. Those wild horses are the most incredible, beautiful creatures in the world. Yeah, we ran alongside them. The wild horses were free. We were free. Me and my Native boys. Free."

He looked over at Dylan. She had tears in her eyes.

"That's the best horse story I've ever heard," she said.

They fell silent for long minutes.

"Okay, you know all about me, Miss Interrogator. Tell me more about you. Tell me why a Kentucky girl moved all the way to Arizona."

"I had a bad marriage. I was young and really naive. I didn't know anything about men or marriage or boyfriends or anything. I'd grown up pretty much on my own because my parents were really busy trying to make a living. They didn't have much time for us. And I told you about how I took care of those five little hellions. My girlfriends from high school lived too far away to see very often other than in school. I was lonely. So when this guy came along, I fell for him. Or more accurately, I fell under his influence."

He nodded to encourage her. "Go on."

Dylan looked at Cass. "Are you sure you want to know all this? It's kind of a typical story. Pretty boring."

"Tell me."

"Okay, so I got married right out of high school. My ex wanted me to be a tattoo artist so I did what he wanted. I did what he wanted most of the time. Too much of the time. I learned how to be a tattoo artist, and I started working at a tattoo place in Lexington. I think my mother was worried about me. She convinced me to enroll in college, and she offered to pay tuition. My ex wasn't happy about that. He considered it a waste of time and money. The fact is he wanted to dominate me and make me do what he wanted all the time. He insisted on having control, and if I did something for myself, he became livid. He wouldn't let it go. He yelled and screamed about the slightest thing, and after a while, I became afraid of him. Emotional abuse. That's what they call what he did. But I enrolled in community college anyway, and, eventually, I got my associate degree. That took a while because I only went part time. When he and I split up, I decided I needed to make a better living and get away from him and everything there and start a new life. So I moved out here, supported myself as a tattoo artist, returned to school, finished my bachelor's degree from the University of Arizona, and I got my CPA license. Now I work for an accounting firm. I get paid much better than I did working as a tattoo artist."

"How did you manage to get away from him?" Cass was fascinated. Maybe it was boring to Dylan, but not to him.

"I tried to get away more than once, but he followed me and forced me to return with him. My brother and my father, and a couple of those naughty boys I used to take care, now grown up, came to my rescue. They ganged up on him, and they told him that I was leaving him. They made it clear that if he tried to stop me or if he followed me, they would 'take care' of him. He got it, and he backed off."

"I'm sorry you had to go through this."

"I think he came to believe that they were really threatening to beat him within an inch of his life. He let go of me, and I was able to escape. First, I came out here to check things out. Then I went home, took what little money I had plus a loan from my parents, and I rented a pickup truck and trailer. Betty and I hit the road. It took us several days to get to Arizona. I wanted to start a new life. And I did just that."

"Good for you. You're brave."

"Actually, I've had to struggle with a bad opinion of myself for getting involved with that loser. I mean, what was wrong with me? I'm still trying to forgive myself. So that explains why sometimes I can be a bit…"

"Pushy?" Cass laughed.

"'Pushy' sounds better than 'bitchy.' So now you really do know everything about me. Do you still like me?"

"I like you even more."

Dylan reached out and took his hand.

Cass squeezed her hand. "Hey, I was thinking. Want to spend some time with me this evening? We could go out to eat and do something after that. Or just hang out?" Cass really wanted to spend more time with her.

"Oh, I wish I could, but I arranged with a friend of mine from our animal welfare group to go check out a rumor about a dog-fighting ring. My friend's name is Chelsea."

"What?" Cass was immediately alarmed. He sat up straight. "A dog-fighting ring?"

"It's supposed to be near Sahuarita, just south of Tucson. We're just going to go take a look."

"No, you're not." He was looking at her and frowning.

"Yes, we are. We need to make sure the ring exists so we can report it. Dog-fighting rings are very abusive to the animals. And illegal."

"Yeah, I know all about that. You're not going."

"Yes, I am."

"No, you are not."

"It's my duty."

Cass shook his head. "You are so naive. They will recognize you for what you are, and you'll never come home again. The very idea is extremely dangerous."

"I have to go."

Damn. So stubborn. He knew that if he didn't watch her, she'd sneak off with her friend.

Cass looked at her hard in the eyes. "Then I'm going with you."

5. The Ring

Dylan and Cass returned Betty and Tornado to the corral and said goodbye to Laurie.

"I'll be back," Cass told her. "I want to work with Tornado some more."

"That's great news. You're welcome back anytime," Laurie responded.

Cass said next to nothing on the drive home.

Dylan spoke first. "I think you are overreacting. We're just going to see if these dog fights even exist. Maybe take some photos. I can use my phone for that. We heard the fights happen in a big barn."

He shook his head. "Like I said, you're being naive. The first thing they will do when you enter is to take your phone and keep it until you leave. Taking photos is forbidden."

"Really?"

"Really."

More silence passed between them.

Finally Cass said, "Look. I understand why you want to verify that this is going on, and why you want to see this shut down. Dog fighting is most definitely illegal. It's a felony. And the fights are really horrific. The FBI has a history of shutting down these dog-fighting operations in Arizona and in other states as well. But a couple of women waltzing into this situation just isn't going to work, unless you want to instantly become a target."

"That's why you want to go with us?"

"Yes. We'll pretend we're there there to participate. Maybe even make a bet."

Dylan grimaced.

"We'll collect as much info as possible and leave without getting any attention directed at us. Then we'll alert my colleagues."

By this time, they had arrived back at the Casa Pacifica apartments. Just after she parked, Dylan's phone rang. She had a brief conversation, then turned to Cass. "That was Chelsea. Something has come up, and she can't go after all. So it's just you and me."

"Any chance you'll reconsider?"

"No, this is too important for me to ignore."

Cass frowned. "But you have to do everything I tell you to do. For your own safety. And for mine. I don't want you to get me shot and killed. Agree?"

Dylan frowned. "Okay. I agree."

"We can pretend we're on a date." He glanced over at Dylan.

Dylan smiled. "Not exactly my idea of a fun date."

"It just means I'll have to kiss you a lot. Just try to be authentic." He smiled.

"It's easy to be authentic. I'll whisper your forbidden word so I can get those kisses."

Cass nodded. "I have to go up to my apartment for a few minutes. Do *not* attempt to run off without me!"

Dylan smiled. "I'll be good. I promise. I think I'll leave my phone at home."

"Excellent idea."

Cass watched Dylan go into her apartment then he entered his. He immediately made a phone call to the local FBI office and explained the situation to his colleague Cory Mardon.

"If it turns out that my informant is correct, you'll have to move fast. They will probably close everything down immediately if they have even a hint we're on to them," Cass said. Mardon immediately agreed.

While he was talking on the phone, Cass found a leather sheath with a strap. "Okay. We'll be leaving here in a few minutes. I gave you her car's description so it will be easy for you to spot us, but be careful when following us. I definitely don't want you to be seen at all or associated with us in any way. Once we get away from there, I'll phone you, and then you and the team can move in." There was a pause, then Cass said, "Yeah, I'll be careful. And you be careful. Out for now."

He pulled his jean pants down and strapped the sheath to his calf. He inserted a knife into the sheath. The blade pointed upwards and knife handle pointed downward toward his ankle. He pulled up and buttoned his jeans, and thrust his hand up the pants leg. He was able to quickly and easily grab the handle and extract the knife. He hoped that there wouldn't be any violent interactions, but if there were, at least he'd have a weapon.

Cass found a burner phone and stuck it into his pants pocket. He put the cell phone he regularly used in his back pocket. And a third phone went into his shirt pocket. He locked his apartment door and went to Dylan's apartment. He knocked lightly.

"Come on in." Dylan had traded her jeans for a flowered cotton skirt that reached to just above her knees. She still had her cowgirl shirt and hat on, and cowboy boots finished her look.

Cass couldn't help but stare. He frowned and sighed. She definitely would attract attention.

"What's wrong?"

"Nothing. You're just so beautiful." He turned and walked to the door. Dylan followed him, grinning.

Five minutes later, they were in Dylan's car. Cass quickly thrust his cell phone under the passenger seat, and soon they were on their way to Sahuarita.

"How did your friend hear about this dog-fighting ring?"

"Chelsea's brother lives in the subdivision we're going to drive through. He saw cars coming and going down a dirt road close to his house. The dirt road led to an old, unoccupied house and a big barn. He's a bird watcher so he got out his best equipment for birding. He has high powered binoculars and something called a spotting scope. For a while, he only saw people coming and going. Then he saw some dogs chained to metal poles outside the barn. The worst thing he saw was a dog thrown out on the ground outside the barn. The dog was all bloody. He figured it was dead. That's when he realized what was going on. He called Chelsea to ask for advice on how to safely report this."

"And you two dummies decided to check it out yourselves." Cass shook his head.

Dylan sighed. "Okay. So we're dumb. I'm glad you're here."

"Listen to me, Dylan. You are not going to like what you see. Try your best to stay detached. Focus on details. Look at how the dogs are kept and managed, which person or persons seem to be in control, and the people in the crowd. But don't get caught staring at anyone. If you get emotional and can't manage being detached, then focus on me. You're going to act like you're mainly into me, and I'm there to bet on the dogs. Got that?"

"I understand. We'll collect information and then what? What are you planning?"

"I'm in law enforcement, remember? Dog-fighting events are illegal. They are often operated by criminal organizations involved in other illegal activities. I'll do my best to bring down this illegal scheme and see the organizers go to jail. That's my job. But not today. It will take an FBI team to deal with this. Not me alone. Not me and definitely not you."

"What about the dogs? I've read that they often fight mainly to please the owners. They are often pit bulls who are usually very affectionate and loyal."

"That's true. Those dogs don't start out as killers. They are trained to fight, and they are rewarded for it. We've found in past cases that when these fighting dogs are rescued, they typically go through an evaluation and rehabilitation program. Usually at least half of them return to a normal life and can be safely adopted. In some cases, it's more than half that are rehabilitated. Their aggression is not toward humans usually. It's toward other dogs. So that's what the rehabilitation people have to work on. Aggression toward other dogs."

"What happens to the ones who are not rehabilitated?"

"They have to be put down. Even worse, there are some dogs that have been used as bait."

"Bait?"

"Yes." He glanced over at Dylan. "I don't want to give you the details about that. It's just downright horrible for a dog used as bait."

Dylan nodded. "This is worse than I thought. You're right. We're dummies."

"Just remember to focus on observing details. And if you can't do that, focus on me."

A few minutes later, Dylan pulled off the highway onto a busy city street, then into a quiet residential neighborhood. She followed the streets to the edge of the subdivision, then turned down a dirt road. She drove at least a mile to what appeared to be an old ranch house in the desert with a big barn behind it. There were several cars parked near the house.

"Park out here so we won't be blocked if we have to leave quickly."

She complied. They exited the car and began walking toward the barn. Cass's demeanor had changed now. He had his arm around Dylan's shoulders, he was looking at her and grinning, then at the barn. He leaned over every few steps and kissed her. Dylan began smiling when she realized that they were putting on an act, and she needed to do her part. She put her arm around him. They were on a date now.

Suddenly Cass felt her stiffen. He followed her gaze. Off to the side of the barn, he could see a small grove of mesquite trees. There were a series of metal bars buried deep in the ground under the trees, and a dog was chained to each metal bar. The bars were just far enough apart that the dogs couldn't reach each other. The dogs were watching the people passing by heading for the barn. Several were barking, and most of them wagged their tails when they saw Cass and Dylan approach.

"Those are the fighting dogs. They'll be taken into the ring when it's their turn," Cass said in a low voice.

Dylan looked up at him and nodded. "I'm observing." She smiled.

"Good," he chuckled. "I knew I could count on you." He kissed her just as they walked into the barn.

A young man was standing behind a small table. "Twenty dollars each to watch. If you want to bet, go over to that table." He gestured toward a nearby table with another young man taking bets. Both of them looked to Cass like they were likely regular drug users. Probably opioids or heroin. Both were very thin with straggling hair and damaged teeth, easily visible when they talked or laughed.

Cass handed over the entrance fee of two twenty dollar bills.

Another man approached, carrying a canvas bag. "Put your phones in here."

Cass dropped his burner phone into the bag. "My girl doesn't have a phone. She didn't bring her purse."

The man nodded and gestured them to enter.

Cass looked around. The barn's air was thick with cigarette smoke. There were probably about forty, maybe fifty, people in the room, mostly men, and almost all were smoking cigarettes. He and Dylan moved in closer. They could see a ring of plywood boards that set the fighting area apart from the crowd. The ring was empty.

Two men approached from opposite sides. Each was leading a pit bull toward the ring. One was tan and white and the other black and white. When the dogs saw each other, they began snarling.

"Any more bets?" one man called out. A couple of hands went up. Cass raised his hand, and he gave the man another twenty dollar bill. The tan-and-white dog got the most bets in his favor because he had a history of winning fights. His body was marked with the scars of past bite marks. The black-and-white dog looked younger and less experienced. Cass bet on the black-and-white dog.

Bets taken, one man called out. "Ready to roll!"

Cass felt Dylan stiffen against him as the dogs attacked each other, growling ferociously. He bent to her and whispered, "Observe." She nodded.

The two dogs, both snarling and growling, threw themselves at each other. They each attempted to get their jaws on the other dog's throat. Blood began to flow. The fight didn't last long, probably only a couple of minutes. The tan dog latched his jaws and fangs on the other dog's throat. The black-and-white dog emitted a squeal and then a whimper. He tried to retreat. The crowd erupted into laughter.

The owner of the tan-and-white dog inserted a thick piece of wood into his dog's jaws to force it to relinquish its hold on the black-and-white dog's throat. That took some real strength to get those strong jaws to detach. The black-and-white dog crawled away, whimpering. Blood was seeping from a wound on his throat and another, deeper, wound on his chest.

Cass felt Dylan trembling against him.

"Okay. We've seen enough." He leaned down and kissed her. Then he took Dylan's hand and led her to the exit door.

On the way out, Cass leaned toward the man who'd taken his entrance fee, and he said in a low voice, "We're leaving. If I want to get laid, I need to find something that she likes, and this ain't it."

The man behind the desk nodded. "I get that. Good luck on getting laid." He laughed.

As they walked away from the barn, they both looked back. A man exited from a side door of the barn and tossed the wounded black-and-white dog out into the side yard. The dog lay still, blood still seeping from his neck and chest.

"Cass, what will happen to that dog? Will they get him medical care?"

"No. He's not a fighter so he has no value to them."

"So he'll just lie there in the dirt?"

"Yes. They will load up him and other losers like him and haul them out into the desert somewhere, and throw them out. Dead or alive. If they are still alive, they'll have a slow, miserable death in the hot sun. The dogs aren't even worth the cost of a bullet."

They had reached Dylan's car. She was sobbing now.

"Okay. I'm driving. Give me your keys." She complied. He drove them at a moderate speed back into the residential subdivision. Then he stopped the car in the shade of a big mesquite tree and retrieved his phone from under the passenger seat. Dylan continued to sob. Tears streamed down her face. He retrieved a handkerchief from his pocket and handed it to her. Dylan wiped away the tears.

Cass made a quick call. "Yes, just as we thought. Big time dog-fighting conspiracy. Okay to move in now. Make it quick."

He leaned over and pulled Dylan into his arms. "I'm sorry you had to see this. I know you love dogs. This had to be really hard on you."

"I'm so stupid," Dylan whispered. "I had no idea." She looked up at him. "You just come along and save me and everybody else. You're amazing."

He chuckled. "Hear those sirens? Here comes the cavalry."

A stream of vehicles was coming toward them at a high rate of speed. There were Pima County Sheriff's Department vehicles with lights on and sirens blaring mixed in with unmarked SUVs. Cass turned to look at their license plates. Yep, U.S. Government plates. Those were the FBI agents.

"The cavalry?"

"FBI agents and Pima County Sheriff's Department officers."

"Will they save the black-and-white dog?"

"If the dog is still alive, it will get medical treatment. Yes, I'd say that dog is really lucky, if it's still alive."

Dylan began to cry again. She squeezed her hands into fists, tears seeping down her face. "I'm so pissed off."

Cass smiled. "That's my girl. Let's go home. I want to retrieve the photos I took."

"What photos?"

"You know they took that burner phone I was carrying. But I had another phone on me with a remote button to take photos."

"You had a phone? Where? I didn't see it."

"I'll show you when we get home."

Dylan followed Cass to his place when they returned to Casa Pacifica apartments. She went directly to the bathroom and washed her face and hands. When she returned, she looked better and had a smile on her face.

"Okay, smarty pants, let's see your camera."

Cass grinned. "It's in plain view. I just took a photo of you."

"You did not," she laughed.

"I just took another photo. You can't see the camera? Come closer."

Dylan approached him. Her eyes began searching his body. Then her eyes shifted to look directly into his eyes, and her hands began to roam over his body.

Cass groaned. "You're touching me. You're such a troublemaker."

She ran her hands over each shoulder and arm. She unbuttoned his shirt and felt his bare chest, then her hands moved around to stroke his back. "Nice," she whispered. "All those muscles." Her hands moved down, and she checked his back pockets. "I can't help myself," she whispered, and she squeezed his butt. "Very nice."

Cass sighed and shook his head. "You're naughty."

"Only with you." Dylan checked his front pockets, then she began moving down his legs, one at a time. When she felt the knife sheathed to his calf, she said, "Oh, this is something. Is this the camera? Please pull up your pants leg."

Cass did as instructed. "I couldn't take a gun to the dog fight so I strapped this knife to my leg. I wanted to have a weapon." He pulled it out of the sheath.

"Good grief." Dylan's tone changed. "Cass, I'm so very sorry. You're right. I'm a dummy for thinking I could go there and take photos and notes and then go report everything to the cops. And that I would get away with that. I know you must think I'm an idiot." She pulled back and began buttoning his shirt. "I'm so sorry to cause you so much trouble."

Cass put his arms around her. "Look at my shirt pocket. The lens on the phone is visible through the button hole on the pocket flap. I can control the phone remotely with a special app."

Dylan's eyes shifted to the pocket. "I totally missed that." She looked into his eyes. "You are very clever."

"I'm a trained and experienced FBI Special Agent." He pulled her closer.

"Although I'll have to say that getting to touch you almost everywhere was a really wonderful experience for me." She giggled.

"Then return the favor sometime soon."

She looked into his eyes. "Really? You want to touch me?"

Hell, yeah! Cass said to himself. He nodded. "Yes, really. But not right now. We have business to take care of first. I need to move the photos over to my laptop. Then I'll forward the photos to my colleagues."

They sat at the dining table, Cass woke up his laptop and transferred the photos to the computer. He opened the file and turned the screen toward Dylan so she could see the photos.

"See those last two photos?" Cass smiled. "That's this really lovely woman I know. She thinks she's an idiot, but in reality, she's very smart."

"Smart? Me?" Dylan was surprised.

"You and your friend and your friend's brother discovered a dog-fighting operation. Then you told me about this. Keep in mind that I'm an FBI agent, and I have a responsibility to stop criminal activity. So you told me, and then you went with me to investigate. The end result of your actions is that this criminal organization has been shut down. So give yourself some credit."

"Oh. I didn't think of it that way."

"That's 'cause you weren't thinking."

Dylan laughed. "But this time I did something right?"

"You did something right." Cass turned back to the laptop, wrote a quick email and sent it with the file of photos to his colleagues in the local FBI office. "In case anyone who was arrested tries to claim that they were not present, these photos will prove otherwise. Want to take a look?"

Dylan gritted her teeth as she opened one photo after another. "There's the guy who threw the black-and-white dog out. I hope he goes to jail." She opened more photos. Suddenly she gasped and pulled away.

"What?" Cass asked, alarmed now.

Dylan pointed to a man standing near the ring's perimeter. Unlike the others watching the fight, many of whom were young, working class men, this man was middle-aged, elegantly dressed in a tan suit, and accompanied by two men in dark suits.

"I know him. He comes into our office fairly frequently to see my boss."

"Really? That's very interesting. Do you know his name?"

"No. I just see him go into my boss's office a couple of times a week, and they close the door."

"I'm pretty sure he's the boss, and this dog fight is his operation. I watched him for a while. Everyone was sucking up to him, and he was giving orders. Those two guys in dark suits behind him are pretty obviously body guards."

"Did he get arrested?" she asked.

"I don't know. Let's find out."

Cass picked up his phone and called the local FBI office.

6. Recognition

Sunday was a warm, sunny, March afternoon. Logan decided to sit outside because soon enough it would be too hot to be outdoors except in the early morning. He was going over his lecture notes for the social ethics class he was teaching at the university. Today was the last day of Spring Break, and his classes started tomorrow, Monday. Same for Charlie. Back to kindergarten. Charlie was taking his nap at the moment.

Shevek the cat appeared from nowhere. He jumped into Logan's lap, settled down and began purring. Logan stared at his notebook while he absently stroked the cat's head and back. He wondered what Zoey was doing. He couldn't get out of his mind what she'd said. He wanted to ask her about it, but he didn't know what to say. Logan tried to concentrate on his lecture notes, but he couldn't stop thinking about her.

"Hi, Logan." Zoey was there, smiling at him.

Logan was so surprised that he dropped his notebook. He scrambled to pick it up. Shevek jumped down and stalked away, obviously annoyed at the interruption.

"Hi. How are you? Sit down." He felt tongue-tied. What should he say? He felt his face getting warm.

"I'm fine. Do you have a minute? I'd like to talk to you about Charlie and sports."

"Sports? Okay. Sure. What about sports?"

"Charlie talks to me a lot, usually when we've been on these outings to find bugs and lizards and birds."

Logan remembered what Cass has said about hot sex and a lizard in the bed. His face was hot now. He took a breath. "Yes, he loves doing those biology things with you."

"Lately he's been talking about sports. He wants to start playing on a team."

"Oh, yeah. I remember. I know he mentioned basketball."

"I thought maybe I should ask you what sports you played when you were growing up. If any, that is. You're such an intellectual. Maybe you didn't play, but if you did, maybe you could help him get started in a sport you're familiar with."

Logan nodded. "That makes sense. Yes, I played sports. It would be fun to play with him and help him learn."

"Seems like you told me you played basketball. Am I right?"

"That's right. And after we went to the Wildcat game, Charlie said he wanted to play basketball."

She nodded. "Any other sports?"

Logan nodded. "Baseball, tennis, track. And soccer."

Zoey's eyebrows went up. "Oh, my gosh. You're an athlete."

"Oh, I wouldn't say that. I just played for fun, and on my high school teams. But I get your point. Maybe I could start introducing him to different sports and see what he likes. I still have some equipment in one of my closets. A tennis racket. A baseball bat and mitt. I could try to find a small mitt for kids. That might be a good place to start."

"I only play soccer so I'm not much help. I was a ballet dancer when I was young, but that's not much help either."

Logan smiled when an image of Zoey in a ballet tutu popped into his head. Lovely. "Maybe we could get him swim lessons this summer. I swim. Do you?"

"Yes. Just for fun, never competitively. Swimming is a good idea. He needs to learn how to swim."

Logan nodded.

Zoey suddenly had a serious expression on her face. "Do you mind me spending so much time with Charlie? Do you think I'm being too intrusive?"

"Certainly not. I trust you completely. Charlie loves spending time with you. And he learns so much." He paused and frowned. "I didn't realize it until you came along, but I think Charlie needs some female energy since he doesn't have a mom." And Logan thought to himself, not for the first time, that maybe Charlie's dad needed some female energy, too.

"It's good for me as well. I was pretty traumatized by my son's death. So spending time with such a sweet young boy helps me deal with my grief."

Logan nodded. "I'm very pleased that you are there for him. And, truth be told, I myself would like to spend more time with you. We're going out on our first date this weekend. Just you and me. I'm really looking forward to that."

"Me, too." She was smiling now.

Charlie appeared suddenly. He was rubbing his eyes, and his hair was rumpled. "Zoey, my daddy is being mean."

Logan groaned. "Is this about that crappy cereal with all that sugar? We have to talk about that again?"

Charlie looked at him and whined, "It tastes good. Everybody at school likes it."

Logan looked at Zoey. "Any chance you can explain why it isn't good for him to be eating that?"

Zoey nodded, smiling. "Charlie, that kind of stuff causes glucose-induced hyperactivity."

"What does that mean?" Charlie sat down next to Zoey and leaned up against her.

"The sugar in the cereal becomes glucose in your blood stream, and in a few minutes, all that glucose makes you get all crazy. You want to bang against the walls and spin around and make funny noises."

"Really? That sounds like fun." Charlie giggled.

"It sounds like fun for a few minutes, and then you start feeling sort of sick and you crash, which means you have no more energy and you feel bad. You might even want to throw up. Want me to show you?"

"Yes! I want to see what happens."

Zoey stood and moved away from where Logan and Charlie were sitting. She pretended to be eating some cereal from a bowl. Then she took the band off her pony tail, shook her hair loose, threw her arms out, and she began running in circles and making funny noises.

Just at that moment, Frida came down the back stairs. "What's going on?" Frida grinned when she saw Zoey.

"Zoey's doing the Crazy Zoey Sugar Dance," Charlie laughed.

"Oh, can I join in?" Frida followed Zoey now, spinning around, waving her arms, and singing something off key.

"Me, too," Charlie called out, and he joined the dance. All three were giggling. But the biggest laughs, more like guffaws, came from Logan.

Zoey looked at Frida and Charlie. "Time for the sugar crash!" She grew limp and fell onto the ground. Frida followed her, laughing. Charlie joined them, still giggling.

Zoey made vomiting motions and sounds, then she fell back groaning. "Oh, I'm so sugar sick. I feel terrible!"

"Me, too!" Frida laughed. She pretended to vomit. "No more sugar for me."

Charlie did his best to mimic the vomiting. "No more sugar for me," he giggled.

Logan was still laughing and clapping now. "Bravo! Bravo!" he called out.

Frida stood up first. "Enough of the sugar crap. Are we going to have Sunday potluck like usual? With good food? Not sugar food."

"Sure," Logan said.

"Then I'm going to the market to get something to cook. Something good. See y'all later." Frida waved goodbye.

Cass appeared. He greeted everyone, then turned to Logan. "Got a few minutes?"

"Yeah. Have a seat." Logan gestured to one of the chairs.

Zoey pulled Charlie up to his feet. "How about if we go to my apartment? I'll give you a snack, and we can talk about what to make for the potluck."

"Okay!" Charlie said. "What kind of snack?"

"How about a banana?"

"Yippie. I love bananas," Charlie said. He took Zoey's hand as they walked away. Zoey turned and smiled at Logan.

Logan waved to her, then he turned to Cass. "What's up?"

"Dylan and I have been having more adventures."

"Uh oh. I hope no one was shot?"

"No. No one was shot." Cass proceeded to tell Logan about their visit to the dog-fighting event, and how Cass was able to get them away before the arrival of the FBI and Sheriff's deputies.

"The team went in and busted almost everyone there. I think my colleague said there were thirty-three arrests."

"I am most relieved to hear that you two got away. And I am very glad to hear the dog fights were shut down. I've heard about those, but I've never seen them," Logan said. "From what I hear, they are really brutal events, especially hard for dog lovers to see."

"That's a good word to describe them. 'Brutal.' Dylan was angry and really upset. She cried a lot."

"Not surprised to hear that. She's an animal lover."

"I surreptitiously took some photos at the event." Cass took his camera from his pocket and handed it to Logan. "Ever seen any of these dudes hanging around here?"

Logan studied the photos then handed the phone back. "No."

"If you do see any of them, especially this guy in the tan suit and his bodyguards, call me immediately."

"Who are they?"

"We're not sure yet. I'm trying to find out now. The problem is that Dylan has seen the tan suit guy at her office meeting with her boss. Several times."

Logan frowned. "So there's some connection. And you don't want Dylan to get mixed up with those dudes?"

"That's right. Dylan works for a small accounting firm. I think she said there's only two accountants, Dylan and her boss, and their secretary-receptionist working there. The firm is actually co-owned by a large Phoenix accounting firm, but locally, they pretty much handle everything themselves. Or I should say her boss handles everything. He's in control because he's the co-owner with the bigger firm. I tend to be suspicious, being in law enforcement most of my adult life. It just seems a very odd coincidence that this man in the tan suit would be seen both at the dog fight and at Dylan's office. I have to find out if there's a connection."

"Did you interact with him at the dog fight?"

"No, he was across from us on the other side of the ring. Dylan didn't notice him because she was watching the dog fight. She was engrossed and completely appalled at what she was seeing. But later, when I showed her the photos, that's when she recognized him. She doesn't know his name."

"Did he notice Dylan?"

"I don't know. I think she would be hard to miss. She was one of a very few women at the fight. She's a beautiful woman and easy to notice. Another question is, if Tan Suit Man saw her, did he connect her to the accounting firm?"

"So you have to find out who he is, what his role is in the dog-fighting ring, and why he's visiting Dylan's boss so often," Logan concluded.

"Exactly. He and Dylan's boss could be co-conspirators in the dog-fight conspiracy. Dylan's boss could be an investor. There could be a considerable number of these fights going on in different locations. Or Tan Suit Man could be engaged in some sort of money laundering at Dylan's accounting firm. These dog fights, especially if there's a bunch of them in different locations, could bring in a substantial amount of money. The criminals have to find a way to clean up the money so that it looks like it comes from legitimate business sources."

Logan nodded. "Looks like there are plenty of ways to engage in illegal activities."

Cass leaned back and put his hands behind his head. He frowned. "It's possible that Dylan knows something, but she doesn't know that she knows something. On top of that, it's a really bad idea for anyone in law enforcement to get personally involved with a potential witness. That's a real problem for me."

"Ah." Logan smiled. "And you're saying that you feel personally involved?"

Cass grimaced. He leaned forward and held his head in his hands. He looked up and said, "Dylan is super stubborn, she wants to have her way all the time, she thinks she's right about everything, and I have to convince her to listen to me. She's really difficult."

"And?" Logan smiled.

"She's beautiful and funny and sweet and sexy as hell. I've tried my best to not fall for her, but I'm definitely in over my head. I find her irresistible." He shook his head and frowned. "I have no reason to think that she is a target or could become a target. But that's what I fear. And I cannot shake this gut feeling that there's something illegal going on with Dylan's accounting firm."

"You've been in law enforcement a long time. Do you think you can trust your gut feeling?"

"Sometimes that's all I have. My gut."

"I get that."

"Earlier today I talked to my chief field officer. I asked him if we could hack into the accounting firm's online books and see if there's anything illegal going on there. Basically, I was told there was no way to do it. At this point, there's nothing to indicate any illegal activity so we have no grounds to get a warrant and do a search. Any hacking had to be off the record, and any evidence found would not be admissible in court. But off the record may be necessary in order for me to get crucial information so I can protect Dylan."

"If you want to go with your gut, and if you are willing to make use of a private investigator with no connections or allegiance to the FBI or local law enforcement, I know someone who could maybe help you with that."

"Oh yeah. Who's that?"

"His name is Frankie Miranda. He's a computer forensics expert currently in a three-year training program to become a licensed private investigator. He's helped us before."

"Give me his contact info. Can I mention your name as my source?"

"Yes. But I think you'll have to pay him for his work, even if this is all off the record."

"No problem. This will come out of my pocket."

"Then maybe your gut will be satisfied."

"Let's hope so. Let's keep this between ourselves, okay?"

"Yes, of course. When you and Dylan come to the pot luck this evening, I'll give you Frankie's contact info. And I won't mention this to anyone."

"Consider it a done deal." Cass got up and started to move away. He turned and said, "Thanks, Logan, for everything."

Logan nodded. "No problem."

Cass turned back and smiled. "By the way, how is the lizard-in-the-bed project going?"

Logan chuckled. "Making progress."

Cass nodded. "Good. See you this evening at the potluck."

He returned to his apartment. Not long after, Dylan knocked on his door. He opened the door.

"Hi, Cass. I came to visit you." She smiled and stepped into his apartment.

A visit? Wonder what she's up to? Cass asked himself. A visit was just fine with him. "Come on in. I have some news for you." They sat together on the sofa.

"First, you and I will probably get a call from the county prosecutor about those three guys that assaulted you. We'll both be asked to testify."

"Fine by me," Dylan said. "I want to see them go to jail."

"Also, I talked to a colleague this morning, and he told me that they made more than thirty arrests when they

busted the dog-fighting ring. The dogs were sent to a rehabilitation center in Phoenix. The people there will eval-
uate the dogs, do their best to dramatically reduce aggres-
sive behavior, and then find them homes once the dogs
are fully rehabilitated."

"That's great news. Do you know anything about that
black-and-white dog? The one that was so hurt and then
thrown out in the dirt?"

"Yeah. A team from the county animal shelter found
him outside, still alive. They took him to get medical care
at the vet's office, then they took him off to the rehab center along with those other dogs chained outside under the
trees."

"Oh, I'm so relieved. I bet he'll be one who gets to start
a new life."

There was a brief pause in the conversation. Cass spoke
first. "Dylan, I've been thinking about you."

"That's nice. I think about you, too."

He couldn't help but be pleased to hear that.

"I've been wondering," Dylan began. "After our ride
yesterday, it seems you have a way with horses. Do you
ever miss that life you had when you were growing up and
when you were a Shadow Wolf? I mean, I bet FBI Special
Agents don't get a lot of opportunities to be out in nature
riding a horse, or training a horse. Don't you miss that?"

"Yeah, I do. Lately I've been missing it a lot. I'm not
sure what to do about that, though." He paused. "But
what about you? I could ask the same thing. You must
spend all day everyday in an office, probably working on
a computer."

Dylan sighed. "Yeah, I get sick of it sometimes." She
folded her hands together in her lap. "Do you want to
hear my plan?"

"You have a plan? Yes, tell me."

"I'm saving money. I've been saving money since I started working full time as an accountant. I'm going to buy a small acreage and open my own stable. I'll provide rides, mainly for kids. And I'll board horses, just like Betty is being boarded. Betty will spend her final years with me. This project probably won't make enough money to support myself, at least not at first. So I'm going to open an accountant's office, part-time only. Maybe two or three days a week. I'll also help small businesses organize their financial records more efficiently, and I'll do their federal and state taxes."

"Sounds really good."

"I did some research. Remember those rowdy boys I told you about? The ones I took care of when I was a teen? One of them has Asperger's syndrome."

"On the autism spectrum?"

"That's right. One Saturday, four of them went off to play softball. The autistic kid, his name is Billy, wasn't invited. He just couldn't keep up with what he was supposed to do on a baseball team. So he stayed with me that day. I took him riding. He loved it. So I'm thinking maybe I'll take kids like Billy, and maybe mentally and physically handicapped kids for rides, as well."

"Excellent idea. Could I add a group to consider?"

"Please do."

"Veterans. Especially those with PTSD. With them, it's called 'equine therapy,' and it's said to be especially successful with veterans who survived combat. That could apply to law enforcement, fire fighters, folks like that, who've been through a hard time."

"Oh, that's a great idea! Thanks!" Dylan smiled broadly. "You survived being wounded in combat and getting shot as a law enforcement agent. Do you have PTSD?"

"No. Not really. I have bad dreams sometimes, but I managed to escape the worst of PTSD. Maybe that's because when I was discharged from the Army, I went back to the rez and started working with the horses again. I had my own Apache equine therapy, in other words."

"I'm so glad you had your own way of dealing with it."

Cass nodded. "Yeah, it worked for me. This project sounds perfect for you. Where will you do this?"

"I've been doing little scouting trips. I don't want to stay close to Tucson or close to the Phoenix metro area. Too much competition. I'm thinking of going up north, close enough to Phoenix to get business, but far enough away that I'll have the life I want."

"Any particular place?"

"Payson is only about an hour from Phoenix. There's some small towns just east of there, which are not far northeast of Phoenix. It's very rural up there with lots of trees and pasture. I think Betty will like it."

Cass nodded. "The landscape is more mountainous and much greener." He was acutely aware that the area she was talking about was very close to the western boundary of the Fort Apache Reservation where he grew up. Only a few miles away.

Dylan reached out and touched his hand. "Thanks for not laughing at me. Everyone that I've told about my plan thinks it will be financially impossible, and I'll end up back in some accounting firm the rest of my life."

"I think it's a good plan. In fact, I bet you could get grants working with those kids and with the vets." And it seemed to Cass that her plan would create the life that he would prefer for himself, too. "But don't you think you'll get lonely? I mean you all by yourself."

"Not if you come and visit me." Dylan smiled. "I know you'll be busy taking down all those criminals, but maybe you could come and visit me occasionally. And help me learn how to train a horse like Tornado."

At that moment, Cass had this strong urge to tell her how much he cared about her, and how he wanted more than an occasional visit. But before he could say anything, Dylan stood up.

"Cass, I'll be back in a minute."

Much to his surprise, she didn't go into the kitchen or bathroom. She went into his bedroom and closed the door.

What the hell was she up to? No telling. He laughed to himself.

Dylan reappeared five minutes later. She was barefoot and dressed only in a t-shirt, Cass's t-shirt, which she must have found in his dresser drawer. She came around the sofa and stood in front of him. He was several inches taller than Dylan so his t-shirt stretched down almost to her knees. The short sleeves ended at her elbows. The t-shirt had slipped off one shoulder.

Cass looked up at her and smiled. "What are you doing?" He was quite certain she had nothing on under his t-shirt.

"Remember when I touched you, and you said for me to return the favor?"

He stood up. "Yes, I did say that, didn't I?"

Dylan smiled. "I'm returning the favor now. You can touch me."

"Come with me." Cass took her hand and led her to his bedroom.

7. Shadow Man

"Dylan, wake up, you lazy girl." Cass leaned over and kissed her. "The potluck is this evening, and we need to make something to eat."

"Oh, yeah. I forgot." She stretched and sighed. "It's your fault. You make me forget everything, and I can't think straight." She looked at him sideways and smiled. "You're good. You know that? You are very good."

"I told you that already, didn't I? Now, get up. I need to ask you some questions." He patted her on her bottom.

"Oh, gosh. What happened to my Apache lover boy? Looks like Cass Cosay, FBI Special Agent, is the one talking to me now."

He laughed. "I'll go make us some coffee."

Dylan pulled herself up from his bed and headed for the shower. Cass made a point of not watching her because he knew he would just get distracted. He headed to his kitchen to start the coffee pot.

Dylan appeared ten minutes later. "I don't really feel like cooking. How about if we go buy something ready to eat at the neighborhood market?"

"Good idea. I don't have anything to cook anyway. But before we go, I need to ask you something." He handed her a cup of hot coffee.

Dylan sat down at the dining table with her coffee. "Ask away, Shadow Man."

"Shadow Man? What does that mean?"

"You know? Apache warrior? Shadow Wolf? FBI spy? A sexy guy who hides in the shadows, then jumps out and rescues everyone, and in the process, he drives all the women crazy with desire? That's my Shadow Man."

Cass laughed. "You're nuts, you know it?"

"Whatever. Ask me a question. I'll try to make my orgasm-fried brain work again. What do you want to know?"

Cass grinned. She really knew how to make him feel good. Don't get distracted, he warned himself.

"I want to know everything about your accounting firm, your clients, what you do, who works there, anything you can think of. And especially, tell me anything you know about that man in the tan suit."

"Okay. I'll try." Dylan sighed. "I told you some of this already, but I'll repeat so you'll know how hard I'm trying to please you." She looked up at him and batted her eyelashes. "Maybe you'll reward me." She grinned.

"I'll reward you as much as you want, but later."

She sighed again. "The firm is co-owned by Bob Hutchins. I don't know for sure how long he has owned his share. I think about three years. The primary owner is a firm in Phoenix, Soladach Investments. Bob had to buy in to be able to open the Tucson office. They gave Bob money to get started, to open the office and buy equipment, hire a secretary, for ads and promotions, all that."

"What does that word 'soladach' mean? Is that the founder's name?"

"No. It's an Irish word. It means 'solid.' You know, like rock solid, trustworthy, safe? The company was established some years ago by a man whose family originally came to the U.S. from Ireland. The Phoenix firm invests in other smaller firms, and not just accounting offices. They are heavily involved in real estate as well. And other investments, too, mainly in Maricopa County."

"How do you know all this?"

"I looked it up before I interviewed for the job. I wanted to appear well informed at the interview."

"What kind of financial arrangement does Hutchins have with Soladach?"

"I'm not entirely sure. He's never given me details, and it's not the sort of thing I could ask him. I've learned from his occasional comments that he has to share a portion of all the Tucson firm's earnings with Soladach, but I don't know what the percentage is. Also he has to repay the money they gave him to open the office in the first place. And hiring me was a risk. In the first year working on his own, he got so many clients, mainly due to the location, that he began to feel overwhelmed. So he got Soladach to agree to hire me. But ultimately, that means that he owes even more money to them for my hire. My job is to handle more clients locally so that we make more money."

"So that he can pay back his debt to Soladach." That is an obvious reason to be focused on increasing income, legally or not, Cass thought to himself.

"That's right. I know Bob worries a lot about money. Sometimes he seems quite anxious, despite the fact that both of us put in a lot of hours."

"I get that. To sum up, he pays a certain percentage of all the Tucson firm's earnings to Soladach. That comes off the top. Then he has this loan he has to pay back to Soladach for opening the firm in the first place. And for you, and you come with risk."

"That's right. And he has to pay salaries to me and Becky."

"Does he have a family?"

"A wife and a couple of kids. They are both teenagers."

"Teenagers can be expensive."

Dylan nodded.

"Who is Becky?"

"Becky Simmons. We call her our office manager. She does a lot of stuff. Receptionist, secretary, keeps track of our records, makes appointments, handles any ads or promos we do to bring in more business, maintains our firm's website. Pretty much everything except the actual accounting work for our clients."

"What do you know about her?"

"She's a single mom with a son in middle school. She's a widow, I think. She's in her fifties. She's very efficient and very friendly. She talks a lot about activities that she's involved in at her church."

"When you say she keeps track of your records, do you mean online records?"

"Yes, we have an online database with folders for each of our clients with all their financial records. The online database keeps track of what we do for each client, how much we bill them for the work, and all that kind of stuff."

"Who has access to the online information?"

"All three of us." Dylan paused. "We're all included in the office network. The folders are organized by their names and dates. When you look inside a folder, you find what kind of work our firm did for the client, how much they were billed, if they paid us or not, all the basic info you keep on a client. Becky has to access those records, too, because she keeps up with making sure everyone pays their invoices on time."

"Have you ever accessed any of the files for clients that Bob handles?"

"No. I've had no need to do that."

"And your office computers can all access these online records? I mean you're all connected to each other in one network?"

"That's right. We have corporate emails as well, that are accessible by everyone. Those emails are always supposed to be about the firm's business, nothing personal."

"Do any of the three of you have another computer that is not hooked into this network?"

"Bob has a laptop I see him carrying around sometime. It's not in the network. I have a laptop, but I leave it at home. It's for my personal use. I assume his laptop is for personal use."

"Now tell me about Tan Suit Man."

"Like I told you, I don't know his name. Becky might know. I'll ask her when I go to work tomorrow. I've never had any interaction with him. Bob never introduced him to me. He comes in frequently, and he goes directly into Bob's office and closes the door."

"And Becky. Does she interact with him?"

"No. Actually that's kind of weird. Becky usually sets up the appointments, welcomes clients to the office, gets them coffee or water, and when it's convenient, Bob often introduces them to me, too. It does seem odd that Mr. Tan Suit is kind of off the radar."

Cass nodded. "Okay. That's all very informative. Now here's what I want you to do."

"Go back to bed without my clothes on?"

He shook his head and laughed. "Try to be patient for now."

"I'm having a hard time being patient."

"Here's what I want you to do. When you go to work tomorrow, ask Becky what Tan Suit's name is. Ask her if she knows anything about him. And when you go into your online network, see if you can find a folder for him.

If there is one, take a look and see if it looks pretty much like a regular record of work being done for him."

"Okay. I'll do that. Will I be rewarded for my effort?"

Cass chuckled. "You are nothing like that quiet, shy woman I first met when I moved into Casa Pacifica."

"I wasn't quiet and shy. Actually whenever I saw you, I was frozen stiff with lust for you. I couldn't talk." Dylan wiggled her eyebrows.

"Oh, yeah? Whatever." He was laughing now. "I think that was me that was frozen with lust for you. Now go put your shoes on. We're going to walk to the market and get something for the potluck."

"You liked me from the beginning? Really?" She sounded surprised.

Cass sat down next to her and took her hand in his. "Yes. Lust from minute one. Then when I got to know you, I realized that you are really special. Going horseback riding with you clinched the deal for me. A woman who loves horses is irresistible."

"This is scary for me." Dylan was frowning now.

"Scary?"

"From the first moment I met you, I found you very attractive," she said. "I wanted to know you better. Then when you rescued me from those bad guys, and you made me laugh, and everything you've done since then made me have much deeper feelings for you. Falling in love is scary."

"Falling in love?" Cass asked. He felt his heart beat faster.

"Yes. I can't help myself. I feel like I'm falling in love with you."

He reached out and took both her hands in his. "May I return the favor? May I return those feelings?"

Dylan's eyes filled with tears. "Oh, that would be the best thing ever. Yes, please return the feelings."

Cass kissed her. "Consider it done. I'm officially falling in love with you, too, Dylan Scott. Now go put your shoes on."

Dylan laughed. "You can be pretty pushy yourself, Shadow Man."

"Go put your shoes on!"

"Okay! Okay!"

* * *

All the tenants in Casa Pacifica attended the Sunday evening potluck at Logan's place. The only exception was traveling photojournalist Marc who was still away from home on a job. Logan looked around the room. Zoey, Frida, Li, Dylan and Cass were all there. And Charlie. Five-year-old Charlie loved the potlucks because he was often the center of attention. Everyone was especially pleased to see Li, the Chinese-American chef, recuperating from a gunshot wound.

"How are you, Li?" Logan asked. Li had been shot in the shoulder by a man bent on taking out former resident Nina Perry and her jazz group, Take Four. Cass, the FBI Special Agent, had arrested the perpetrator, and Li had been recuperating from the wound.

"Doing well, thank you," Li smiled. "I went back to work this past week. If I stayed away too long, everyone in the kitchen would try to transform authentic Chinese food into authentic Mexican food."

"You have mostly Mexican Americans workers in your kitchen?" Logan asked.

"Yes. I think that's the case for a lot of Tucson's restaurants. I'm trying my best to convert them to Chinese."

Logan noticed that Cass and Dylan were standing very close to each other. They frequently exchanged glances and smiles. Logan was happy to see this. His gaze went to Zoey. Okay, he had to admit it. Zoey made him happy as well. And Charlie. She made Charlie very happy, especially when she danced the Crazy Zoey Sugar Dance. Charlie had demanded that she dance the sugar dance again, and of course, he had to join in. But thankfully, Charlie seemed to have forgotten about that crappy sugar-covered cereal that he had been so intent on stuffing down his throat. Logan hoped he would forget it forever.

They ate their dinner, chatting the entire time. Charlie dominated the conversation with tales about his kindergarten experiences and his adventures with Zoey. Everyone smiled and laughed. It was obvious that they all had a lot of affection for the only child at Casa Pacific apartments.

Dinner was over, the table cleared, and Logan went off to put Charlie to bed. When he returned, he said, "Before you go, I'd like to run a couple of things by you."

Everyone gathered around, now seated comfortably on the sofa or in stuffed chairs.

"As you know, we had this trouble with that loser who was trying to exact revenge by smashing the bones in Nina's hands and making it impossible to play her piano anymore." Logan glanced over at Zoey. "And he hit Zoey."

Everyone nodded, serious now.

"I'd like to thank Zoey again. She made it possible for Charlie to escape that jerk. Thank you, Zoey." She nodded and smiled. "And I'd like to thank Cass again for showing up at just the right time, disarming the guy, and arresting him." Cass nodded. Logan noticed that Dylan squeezed his hand.

"Our neighborhood is usually pretty quiet, and relatively crime free considering how close we are to Fourth Avenue, to the university and all that. But this business with Nina isn't the only thing that has happened lately. Did everyone hear about how Dylan was attacked and assaulted?"

Everyone nodded, again serious.

"And Cass rescued her as well."

Dylan leaned up and kissed him. Everyone grinned, and Logan could hear Frida chuckling.

"So we need to be watching for anything odd or unusual, especially watching for people new to the neighborhood who seem to be focused on our apartment building for no apparent reason. I'm going to start locking both the front and kitchen-laundry door, as well as the door to the back yard. I mean these doors will be locked all the time, not just at night. And of course, keep the door to your apartment locked."

"What happened to those dudes who attacked Dylan?" Frida asked.

Cass answered. "They're in the county jail. They were arrested in Santa Cruz County for speeding, running for the border. Authorities brought them here to Pima County, and now they are awaiting trial. Dylan and I will both be testifying."

Logan pulled the letter out of his pocket. "Okay. That takes care of the serious stuff. Now here's something you will all enjoy. I have a letter from Nina."

"Oh, goody," Frida said. "I can't wait to hear what she's been up to. Does she like Vancouver?"

"Yes," Logan said. "I'm going to read it now."

Logan, please read this to all my pals at Casa Pacifica.

Dear Everyone. Hi! First, the important stuff. I love, love, love Vancouver. It has to be the most beautiful city in the world. And I love, love, love Gwilym Sanjay Havard even more than I love Vancouver. I am happier than I've ever been in my life.

I've been really busy. As you know, Gwilym has a jazz club and a book store. I'm playing regularly in the club. Sometimes I play alone and sometimes with some local cats who have formed a sort of informal group with me. Gwilym had a bunch of dates already taken on the calendar with touring jazz musicians, and I often get to jam with them, too. I cannot tell you how pleasurable this has been for me.

And here's the really great news! Gwilym helped me get in contact with a record producer. I signed a contract with the producer, and I recorded an album of me playing the piano solo and me singing a couple of tunes. The title of the album is India Eyes. *I wrote this tune and named it after my darling Gwilym who has the sexiest eyes of any human being on planet earth. I tell him that often, and that always makes him laugh. He thinks I'm silly, but I know he's pleased.*

I also help out in his bookstore. I don't work there, but I act in an advisory role to help build up the music section. That's fun. What else? We often go to this big park, Stanley Park. We go do things like hiking, and we went out on a boat. It has some special name. The boat, I mean. I know nothing about boats. But the landscape is lovely with all that water and the mountains and the beautiful city of Vancouver. We've been exploring, too. Once we went over to Vancouver Island. It's a beautiful place.

When am I coming back to Tucson? Gwilym says any time I want. I think we'll wait until the fall when it's not so hot in the Old Pueblo. And we'll be back for sure for the jazz festival in January.

Okay. That's about all from the lovely city of Vancouver from your friend.

Oh, one more thing.

Logan looked at his friends. "This last bit is sort of embarrassing, but I'll read it anyway." He returned to the letter.

And finally, Logan! Have you asked Zoey out yet? If not, do it! Don't be shy!

Everyone laughed. Logan's face was pink now, and Zoey's face was pink as well.

Logan looked around the room at everyone. "For the record, I am not shy. I did ask Zoey for a date, and she said yes. We're going out Saturday evening."

Zoey nodded her confirmation. "Logan is not shy. He's thoughtful."

"Thank you, Zoey. Okay. Here's the last bit from Nina." Logan looked at all of them then back to the letter. "This is for Charlie. I'll read this to him tomorrow."

Tell Charlie I love him the most, and I miss him the most. Tell Charlie I'll see him in a few months. Love to you all, Nina Who Is Feelin' Good.

Logan folded the letter and put it in his pocket. "Thanks for coming, everyone. Have a good week."

Just before Cass left, Logan slipped him a piece of paper. "Frankie Miranda's contact info."

Cass nodded, then he, Dylan, Frida, and Li waved goodbye. Zoey lingered. "We have a busy week ahead of us, Logan, since school starts again tomorrow. I'd like a little goodnight kiss, please."

Logan kissed her, but it wasn't a little kiss. Zoey finally pulled away from him, smiling, and she went to the door. He followed her and watched her walk to her apartment. She turned and waved just before she went in and closed her door behind her. Logan closed his door, too. He felt really great, the best he'd felt in a long, long time.

8. The Laptop

The next morning, Dylan and Cass sat at his table drinking coffee and eating breakfast.

"I like it that you are staying overnight with me," Cass said.

"I like it, too. Your bed is very sexy."

"My bed, huh? Not me?"

Dylan looked up at the ceiling, a pensive look on her face. "Hmm...maybe it is you, not your bed. Yeah, you're the one who's sexy."

"That's a relief. Is this omelet going to be enough for you?"

"Definitely. I'm not used to being waited on like this."

"Waited on?" he chuckled. "There's a price you'll have to pay for my service."

"Oh, yeah? What kind of price?"

"You have to go horseback riding with me again. Soon."

"That's a treat, not a price to pay. I would love to go riding with you again soon. You can work a little more with that bad boy, Tornado."

Cass nodded. "That's what I had in mind. I want him to behave and stop nipping Betty."

"Betty likes you. Betty likes your carrots and apples. Betty likes that you are training Tornado. Betty likes it that you make me happy."

Cass sipped his coffee. He liked knowing that Betty approved of him.

"I have a question for you," Dylan said.

"What's that?"

"Tell me your full name. Do you have a middle name? Is your name an Apache name? Just tell me all about your name."

"My name is Cassadore Cosay. No middle name. Cosay is a common surname on the White Mountain Apache rez where I grew up."

"What does Cassadore mean?"

"Cassadore is the name of a nineteenth-century Apache warrior and chief. There's also a Cassadore Mountain located on the San Carlos Apache reservation northeast of Globe, Arizona."

"Oh, can we go horseback riding there someday?"

Cass smiled. "Sure. What about you? Your name, I mean."

"Dylan Marie Scott. Dylan is my mother's family name. And Marie is my grandmother's name. Scott is for those who came originally from Scotland." She shrugged her shoulders and smiled. "My dad's family came from Scotland."

Cass nodded. He sipped more coffee, then he said, "Okay. Time to get serious."

"Oh, you want a quickie before I go to work?"

Cass laughed. "Not that kind of serious. What I mean is this. When you get to work, ask your office manager if she knows the name of Tan Suit Man. If you get a name, text it to me first. Then look him up in your database of files. Open those files, and take a good look. See if you can find any irregularities in his accounts."

"Irregularities? Anything in particular?"

"You're the accountant so you'll notice if something sticks out as weird. But I am particularly interested in knowing where funds come from. I mean funds being deposited into the account. I'd like a general idea of how much is deposited, large amounts or small amounts? Are deposits regular or irregular? Is there another bank or business where the funds are coming from on a regular basis?"

"Okay. And you probably want to know the same kind of information about any funds going out of the account?"

"Yes. Do they go out to only one account or more than one, and where? Same kind of info. Look for anything irregular."

"Okay. Will this make me a Special Investigator for the FBI?"

"Special Agent, not Special Investigator. And no, it won't make you an FBI Special Agent. You have to sleep with your supervisor to get that designation."

Dylan grinned. "And who would be my supervisor?"

"Me, of course."

That made Dylan laugh out loud. "That's illegal, you know?" She giggled.

"This is a special case, calling for special...uh...arrangements."

"Very well. Consider me on the job. Of course, I can't report to my supervisor unless we have a *very* special arrangement."

"And what would that be?" Cass found her very amusing.

Dylan leaned forward and whispered in his ear.

"Oh, you naughty girl." He laughed.

Cass stood up and carried their dishes to the kitchen. He turned and smiled at her. "Enough of this. I'm going to walk you to work now. I'll be there at noon to meet you, and we'll go for lunch. Don't forget to text me right away if you get a name for Tan Suit Man."

"Yes, sir. You're very handsome, you know."

"I'm not handsome. I'm kind of rough looking."

"Yeah," she grinned. "I like your dark eyes, your high cheekbones and your nose."

"My big hook nose?"

"The proper term is 'aquiline.' You have an aquiline nose. Just like the president of France, Emmanuel Macron. He has an aquiline nose, too. He's very handsome."

Cass shook his head and chuckled. "Yeah, me and Macron. Apache men and French men have so much in common."

"When it comes to male beauty, you do." Dylan nodded her head firmly. "I'm an expert on the subject of male beauty. Don't argue with me."

"Perish the thought that I might argue with you. Now go get ready. I'll escort you to your workplace."

Cass left Dylan at the entrance to her office, and then he walked home. Only a few minutes after his arrival, he received a text from Dylan.

Becky says Tan Suit Man is Raul Ortega. I looked, but no folder for him in the directory under that name.

Cass texted her back. *If you learn more, text or call me. See you at lunch.*

She replied, *You're so handsome.*

You're so beautiful. I'm not so handsome. Now shut up and go back to work.

Dylan's final text was an emoji of a smiling face and, *Don't forget. I'm an expert in male beauty.*

Cass decided to take this free time to work on his fitness. He went on a five-mile jog to the University of Arizona campus and back again. After a shower, he spent time on his computer looking up typical crimes associated with accounting firms. He found quite a bit of information on the topic, and, in particular, he read about various forms of fraud and other deceptive practices. He just couldn't shake the notion that something illegal could be happening at Dylan's firm. But before he could go forward, he had to determine the identity of Tan Suit Man, or Raul Ortega, if that was his real name.

Time to meet Dylan for lunch. Cass walked briskly to Fourth Avenue and waited for her across the street from her office. She was late. He was seriously considering going into her office when she finally appeared. She wasn't the usual smiling woman he was accustomed to seeing. Now Dylan was looking worried. She didn't smile when she approached Cass.

"What's wrong?" he asked her.

"Cass, something weird is going on. When I went into the office this morning, Becky told me that Bob, my boss, took a phone call early, then he came out of his office in a hurry. He put a laptop computer in the big side-drawer of my desk. Becky said that Bob told her to tell me to take care of his laptop. A few minutes later, Raul Ortega, the one you call Tan Suit Man, showed up with one of his men and went directly into Bob's office. When all three came out, Becky said that Bob looked scared. He didn't say anything to Becky, just glanced back briefly."

"You found the laptop in your desk drawer?"

"Yes. But I didn't look at it. I had an appointment with a client right then. The client showed up, and I spent time with him going over his taxes. I had two additional clients this morning, too. Becky left for lunch a few minutes ago. She's taking the afternoon off because she has a doctor's appointment. So I locked the office so no one could come in while I was there alone. I don't have any clients coming in this afternoon so I'm going to lock the entrance door to the office, put out the 'Closed' sign and just work alone."

"I'll be there to meet you at the end of the day. And you can text or call me if you want to leave early."

"I'll feel safer if I can be with you."

"Want me to stay with you in your office this afternoon?"

"No. Closing the office makes it look like no one is there. I can work in peace. Just be here at the end of the day and walk home with me."

"I will. What about the laptop?"

"It's in my tote bag." She had her purse and her tote bag hanging from her right shoulder.

Cass took the tote bag from her. "Okay. Let's go home and eat lunch." Cass put his arm around Dylan's shoulder. "Everything is going to be just fine."

When they arrived back at Casa Pacifica, Cass kissed her. "What do you want for lunch?"

"I have some leftover chicken salad in my fridge. I'll go get it."

"I'll go with you." He'd already decided that he wasn't going to let Dylan out of his sight. Hearing about her boss leaving hurriedly with Tan Suit Man was concerning to Cass. Something was going on. He was sure about that.

They went to Dylan's close-by apartment, retrieved the chicken salad and went back to Cass's place. He made them sandwiches, and they ate.

"I'm going to make a call," Cass said. He pulled out his phone and called the number that Logan had given him. He spoke for a few minutes, then hung up. He turned to Dylan. "There's a computer forensics expert coming here later this afternoon. He'll be able to tell us if there's anything peculiar on your boss's laptop. I know you will probably be able to see if something is wrong with the accounts, but it won't hurt to get some expert advice."

"Makes sense to me. I never made a point of learning how to commit an accounting crime, so I'm not sure I would recognize one if I saw it."

They sat together on Cass's sofa.

"Sure you don't want to stay here this afternoon?" he asked.

"I'd like to but it's tax season. I have a lot of work to do before the April 15 deadline. Being there alone all afternoon with no clients means I'll be able to catch up some on the work. I'm so glad you're here, Cass. I wouldn't know what to do if I were on my own. That whole dog-fighting ring was so awful. And now my boss has gone off for some reason, and leaving his laptop with me is very strange. I don't know what's going on."

Cass put his arm around her and pulled her close. "I meant it when I said everything is going to be okay. We'll get to the bottom of this. Try to stop worrying."

They sat together for a while in silence. Then Dylan said, "I have to go back to work. Walk with me, okay?"

Cass and Dylan returned to her office. He went from room to room to make sure no one was there. When she locked the entrance door, he stood just outside to make sure he could not get in without breaking the glass or the lock. He waved goodbye to her through the glass. Dylan went back to her computer, and Cass returned to his apartment.

The first thing he did upon arrival was to open the laptop and see if he could access any files. However, the laptop was password protected, and he couldn't get past the opening page. He went to his own computer and began a search for Raul Ortega. The name was a fairly common Hispanic name, but none of the names he found seemed relevant. An athlete, a musician, a scientist, the list of Raul Ortegas was fairly long. Many entries had photos, but no photo matched the Tan Suit Man. Probably the name was an alias. Cass figured it would be up to him to discover the man's real name.

Cass sat back and thought about his resources. The FBI had an extensive lists of individuals' rap sheets, which included arrest records, fingerprints, personal information such as immigration status, military service, and the like. Also there was the National Crime Information Center which included state and local law enforcement information as well as FBI and federal info. But he had nothing to go on but visual identification from a photo and it wasn't even a mug shot. He'd taken the photo across a smoke-filled barn with a crowd watching dogs fighting to the death. He needed more information.

Cass had been searching for about an hour when he received a text from Dylan.

I can't concentrate, Cass. I'm sort of scared. Do you mind coming to pick me up? I don't want to walk home alone.

"Sort of scared" meant Dylan was terrified. Cass responded immediately.

I'll be right there. Don't open the entrance door until you see me.

She responded. *I love you, Shadow Man.*

Likewise, Smarty Pants. Now shut up and look out for me. I'm coming.

She responded with a laughing emoji. *You're coming? You couldn't wait for me? Naughty boy.*

Cass sighed. She was going to be a real handful. He put the computer to sleep, locked his apartment door, and set off at a semi-run to Fourth Avenue. When he arrived at Dylan's office, he found her standing back from the door, looking very anxious. She immediately unlocked the door, came out, and locked the door behind her. Cass took her hand in his, and they headed home.

Later that afternoon, Frankie Miranda showed up at Cass's apartment. Cass opened the door to his knock and stood back so he could enter.

Dylan looked up and grinned. "Hey, Frankie!"

"Hello, Dylan. What are you up to? Here to give Mr. Cosay a tattoo? I heard you quit the business."

"I did quit, but I'm thinking about putting my brand on Cass." She laughed.

Cass shook his head. "Don't listen to her. She's a smart ass. And you can call me Cass. How do you two know each other?"

Frankie pulled away his t-shirt from his neck. "Dylan did this." He pointed to a Chinese character on his neck. "It says 'courage.'"

"I see," Cass said. "Dylan is an accountant now. Change of professions."

"I changed professions, too," Frankie said. "I went from grocery store clerk to private investigator specializing in computer forensics."

"Excellent," Dylan responded. "Cass will fill you in on what our problem is."

"Our interactions are confidential, right?" Cass asked.

"Definitely. Completely confidential."

Cass pointed to the laptop. "We need to get into this computer and look at some files. But it's password protected."

"No problem," Frankie said. He sat down, opened the laptop and began working. He attached a cord from his own laptop to the one Dylan had acquired. A few minutes later, Frankie said, "I'm in. What are you looking for?"

"A file folder labeled Raul Ortega," Cass answered.

Frankie searched for the folder. "Easy peasy. Want to look inside?"

"Yes. Tell me what you're finding."

"Okay. There are several interior folders in the main Ortega folder." Frankie paused. "Each interior folder has a different name. Inside are records of transactions, both funds coming in and funds going out."

"What do you mean, each folder has a different name?" Cass asked. "The name of a business?"

"No. I mean literally a person's name. Raul Ortega is the name of the entire folder, but the interior folders have other personal names. Examples are 'Francesca,' 'Igor, ' 'Ahmad.' Only first names. No surnames."

"When you look inside a folder, what do you find?"

Frankie continued clicking. "It appears that each personal name represents a bank account. There's a record of money coming in, deposits, I mean, and money going out."

"Check each folder and see where the money is coming from." Cass said.

Dylan was looking over Frankie's shoulder as he went from folder to folder.

"It appears each deposit is coming from a couple of banks in Phoenix," Frankie said.

"Big, well-known banks," Dylan added. "Not one that would attract attention or be considered suspicious."

"What is the source of the money that goes into the Phoenix banks?" Cass asked.

"That's fairly complicated because it looks like there are numerous sources, primarily in cash-intensive businesses. Examples I see here are car washes, arcades, restaurants, and bars. These smaller businesses are in several towns around Arizona and New Mexico. And there's one in Utah, too. Cash is deposited into one of the Phoenix bank accounts. Since it's cash, the origin is harder to trace. It's likely that there are only a few sources, and they are channeling it through these cash-intensive businesses. I can't tell for sure what the ultimate origins are."

"Okay. How about where the money goes?" Cass asked.

"Give me a few minutes." Frankie returned to the folders. "I just compared two folders. One is Francesca's and the other is Igor's. Money goes out in set amounts, usually ten thousand U.S. dollars each time, and then it is deposited into off-shore banks."

"The name of the account for the offshore banks?" Cass asked.

"Only two names for these accounts, not a long list of depositors." Frankie fell silent for a few minutes. "Ah. I see." He clicked on additional folders. "Once a deposit has left the Phoenix bank, it goes into one of these off-shore banks. Switzerland is a popular destination. The funds are then sent off again, usually in larger amounts, this time to a bank in Saudi Arabia." He clicked on more folders. "Okay, looks like after several deposits and withdrawals, the money is all ending up in one bank account in Riyadh, Saudi Arabia. The owner of the account is a man named Ahmad Ahmad." Frankie continued clicking. "Yep. Looks like the other folders follow the same procedure."

"Money laundering," Cass said.

"Oh, my god," Dylan groaned. "My boss was facilitating an illegal money laundering scheme."

Cass nodded. "I think when we look into this, the dog-fighting rings are just one of the income sources for Raul Ortega, or whatever his name really is. I doubt the dog fighting would bring in a huge amount of money. Maybe watching dogs trying to kill each other is just a personal interest of Ahmad's, assuming he's the one who ends up with all the money." He paused. "Do you have any ideas about how to definitely identify this man going by the name Raul Ortega, but who is collecting big bucks in Saudi Arabia under the name Ahmad Ahmad? I have a photo of him."

"We can try Interpol." Frankie pulled up the website. "The International Criminal Police Organization. We'll look at the Red Notices. There are photographs for each wanted criminal."

"Oh, gosh," Dylan said. "There are nearly seven thousand listed."

"We'll narrow it down." Frankie typed in some parameters. "I'll try the Saudi name first. That's more likely." Frankie scrolled through several pages as they all looked at the photos.

Cass grinned. "There he is! That's the man we saw at the dog fight. Do you agree, Dylan?"

"Yes, that's him for sure," she said.

"So Raul Ortega is really a Saudi national named Ahmad Ahmad."

"Yes, that's right. Give me a minute. Here's a folder that's different." He pointed to the last folder in the list. "This folder labeled 'Roberto' is not like the others. Instead of ending up in Riyadh, the funds go into a bank in Los Angeles. And then the money comes back to Tucson. The account in the Tucson bank is under the name Robert Hutchins."

Dylan gasped. "That's my boss!"

Cass looked at Dylan. "Not only was he money laundering a criminal's illegal funds, he was skimming off some money for himself."

"Oh, boy," Frankie said. "If Ahmad finds out that Hutchins was stealing money from him, there will be hell to pay."

"Yeah, we think that is what's happening now," Cass said to Frankie. Cass looked at Dylan. "Those goons came to get your boss, but just before they arrived, he put this laptop in your desk drawer. He knew he was in deep shit. I bet he was hoping you'd figure out what was going on and rescue his ass."

Dylan's eyes filled with tears. "I don't know what to do."

"I'm taking over and contacting my colleagues. The FBI can handle this." Cass stuck his hand out to Frankie. "Well done, man."

Frankie smiled, very pleased. "My pleasure. Actually this is pretty much fun for me. I like solving this kind of puzzle. I'll send you an invoice from Valdez Investigations."

"Excellent. I'll pay you right away. You may be called on as an information source for the FBI investigation, and later, you may be called on to testify in a trial."

"Letty will like this," Frankie said. "I want her to have complete confidence in me."

"Oh, I'm sure she does," Cass said. "Is she still off surfing with her new husband? I'd like to meet Letty Valdez."

"No, Dan took her to Buenos Aires. Now they're taking tango lessons." Frankie shook his head and laughed.

Cass turned to Dylan. "We need to get Bob Hutchins's wife to contact the police and report her husband missing. That will get the ball rolling. Meanwhile, I'll get the FBI in on this, and I'll text Logan and update him. And, as for you, Dylan Scott, I'm sticking to you like glue."

9. TROUBLE

As soon as Frankie had gone, Cass called the Tucson FBI office and asked to speak to his most trusted colleague and best friend there, Cory Mardon. Cass explained what was going on. "Yeah, I have the laptop computer with all the info on it. I can give you the password to get in plus what to look for in each of the folders. All the money ends up in a Saudi Arabian bank, except for one folder. That money comes back to Tucson. Looks like the accountant doing the money laundering was skimming off some for himself." There was a pause. "Yeah, I hope we can get to him before they kill the accountant."

Dylan's eyes went wide then filled with tears.

"Okay, Cory. I'll bring the laptop to you first thing in the morning. Too bad your FBI computer forensics guy doesn't work at night." He laughed. "Yeah, yeah, I know. They don't pay us enough to work twenty-four hours a day, do they?" He and Mardon exchanged a few more words, then he said goodbye.

Dylan was sitting on the sofa so Cass came to sit beside her. To him, Dylan looked very distressed.

"Do you really think they would try to kill Bob?" Her voice was wavering.

"Yes. From what Frankie found, this guy Ahmad is a big time criminal. Interpol has him listed in the Red Notices, and that's serious. He very likely has no patience at all for people who are supposed to be working *for* him and then make the very big mistake of stealing money *from* him."

"Ahmad will throw Bob away just like he throws away those wounded dogs." She wiped away tears. "Bob's not a bad guy. He just got in over his head financially."

"That's right. Ahmad won't have any sympathy for him. We need to get a missing person's report out on Bob. I suggest you call his wife now. See if she knows anything."

Dylan found her phone. "Hi Jessica. I'm calling to see if Bob is there. He left the office this morning, and Becky and I haven't heard from him since." Dylan fell silent for several long minutes. "Okay. Yes, I think that was a very good idea to call the police. Please call me if you hear anything. Talk to you soon."

Dylan disconnected. "Jessica is worried sick. She said that Bob was supposed to come home at noon and go with her to the high school to have a parent-teacher conference about one of their kids. But Bob never showed up. She's tried calling and texting him, and he doesn't respond. She called the police about an hour ago and reported him missing."

"Good. That gets the ball rolling. It's best that his wife be the one who reports him. She's the one most familiar with his schedule and his whereabouts."

"What about tomorrow? I need to prepare my clients' tax returns. The filing deadline is coming up."

"No, Dylan. Too dangerous for you to go to your office. If Ahmad finds out that there are financial records on that laptop, he'll want to get access to it and destroy it. He could very well return to your office, and look for the laptop. I don't want him to find you there."

"But how could Ahmad know about the laptop?"

The expression on Cass's face was sad. She was so sweet, so naive.

Dylan looked at him, then awareness grew on her features. "Oh, god. Ahmad will do something terrible. He'll force Bob to tell him."

Cass nodded. "Yes, either hurt Bob directly, or threaten Bob's family. Whatever works. So no going into work for you tomorrow, and I think you should call your office manager. Tell her Bob is missing, you're afraid to go into the office in case Ortega-Ahmad shows up again, and you think she shouldn't go in either. In other words, your accounting firm's office will be closed tomorrow."

Dylan grew quiet for a while. "I wish I could go horseback riding right now. That would be such a relief."

"I wish I could go riding with you, too."

She looked at him. "When this is over, let's put our heads together and come up with a plan."

Cass smiled. "Good idea. Let's start now. What's the first step in the plan?"

"We could decide we want to be together." She looked at him, then she looked down at her hands. Cass thought she looked even more afraid of what he'd say in response to that comment than of confronting Ahmad.

Cass put his arm around her shoulders. "I've already decided that. I want to be with you."

"I want to be with you, Cass."

"Next step?" he said gently.

"We have to find a place for our horse farm."

"Looking will be fun. We'll take a drive and go exploring that area you mentioned east of Payson. We can also check out the Fort Apache reservation where I grew up. It's very close."

"They will allow me on the reservation?"

Cass laughed. "You don't have to be Apache to visit the rez. Remember that you'll be with me. I'm a White Mountain Apache enrolled tribal member."

Dylan looked relieved. "I would very much like to see where you grew up."

"Next step?"

"I'm not sure. Looking for a good place was as far as I got. Maybe think about what kind of barn we need. And when we do these equine therapies sessions, where will our clients stay?" Dylan sighed.

"Don't worry. We'll figure it out. But for now, I suggest you call your office manager, Becky, and I'll see if I can find something for us to eat. You're staying with me from now on. If you need anything from your apartment, I'll go with you to get it. Later, we'll go tell Logan about all this. Then he'll know to watch out for Ahmad and his goons."

Dylan called Becky, and Cass texted his FBI colleague Cory Mardon to let him know there was a missing persons alert out for Bob Hutchins. Then he and Dylan ate a quick meal. Next, they went downstairs to let Logan know what was going on. Charlie was watching cartoons and drawing at the same time. The adults sat at the large dining table where they met for potlucks.

Cass again showed Logan the photo of Ahmad that he'd shown him earlier. Cass explained what was going on. "This photo is of a man named Ahmad Ahmad. He goes locally by the name Raul Ortega. He's the mastermind behind a criminal ring, and he's wanted by Interpol. Frankie found information on a laptop computer that will bring him down for his crimes, which involve money laundering through Dylan's accounting firm. I'm taking the laptop into my FBI office and handing it over to them. I don't know if Ahmad knows about how much we know, or if he knows that Dylan lives here. But I'm not taking any chances."

Logan listened carefully. When he spoke, he looked at Cass with a serious expression on his face. "My main concern is that everyone stay safe, especially my son. Li and Frida are often gone during the day, and both work in the evenings, so I don't think they will be here anyway in case this guy shows up. Zoey is picking up Charlie from kindergarten, and he's going with her and her high school biology class on a field trip. They're going to the Flandrau Science Center and Planetarium on the University of Arizona campus. So she won't back here with Charlie until late afternoon. If you encounter a problem, please text Zoey and ask her to keep Charlie in her apartment and make sure he stays busy. She knows how to distract him so he'll stay happy and safe with her. I'll be sure to tell her about this development."

Cass pulled out his phone, and he added both Logan and Zoey's number.

"I already have your number, Cass," Logan said. "I'll let you know if anything happens."

"Good. Maybe we can get this resolved quickly. The local cops and the FBI are working on this now."

Cass and Dylan returned to his apartment.

"We have the evening free. Let's try to relax," Cass said. "Tomorrow the Tucson police, the Pima County Sheriff's Department, and the local FBI officials all will be looking for both Ahmad and Bob Hutchins. I hope you and I can stay out of this."

Dylan nodded. "I think I know a good way to relax." She looked at him and smiled. She directed her gaze at his bedroom door.

Cass grinned. "Oh, so you want your brain fried again."

"Yes, please.

"Very well. Come with me."

* * *

The next morning, Cass said, "Look, I have to leave you for a little while. I'm taking Bob Hutchins's laptop into my local FBI office so they can verify everything that Frankie told us. I don't expect to be gone more than an hour or an hour and a half."

"Before you leave, can we go to my apartment? I want to get my briefcase and laptop and bring them back here. My briefcase has some clients' papers, and I can access the firm's accounting network on my laptop. That way, I can continue working. And I need some clean clothes. And my hairbrush."

"Okay. Let's go get whatever you need."

They returned to Cass's apartment within fifteen minutes.

"I'm going now," he said to her. "Promise me you won't leave my apartment. And if anyone comes here and knocks on the door, don't answer. Promise."

"I promise. Cross my heart."

Cass left Dylan very reluctantly. He was right to follow his gut feeling about something wrong at Dylan's accounting firm. He had this gut feeling now that he needed to be there to protect her. He would do his best to return quickly. He called a taxi and went directly to the FBI office. When he arrived, he texted Dylan.

Everything okay?
Yes, Shadow Man. I miss you.
I'll be back soon.

* * *

Later in the day, it was Logan's turn to teach a one-time seminar in business ethics. Unfortunately, the seminar time conflicted with the time to pick up Charlie from kindergarten. That's just one reason why he agreed to Charlie going with Zoey's biology class to the Flandrau

Science Center. That, and the absolute certainty that Charlie would have the time of his life. The Center would be captivating, he would no doubt get a lot of attention from Zoey's students, and perhaps best of all, Charlie would be with Zoey. He loved being with Zoey. He didn't have to worry about Charlie when he was with her. For now, Logan decided to be disciplined and continue reading his students' essays.

After an hour or so of reading those essays, Logan decided to take a break. He thought about Zoey's comments regarding Charlie's participation in sports. So he went into his bedroom closet to see what he could find. At the very back of the closet, upright in the corner, was a baseball bat. Next to the bat, he found a tennis racket in bad shape. It needed to be restrung. On the top shelf of the closet crammed in the back was a baseball mitt. He brought all three pieces of equipment out into the living room. Memories of his experiences playing sports came to him. Yes, he'd had a lot of fun. And it would be fun now to play some sport with Charlie. And play with Zoey, too. He picked up the bat and starting practice swinging. Maybe he could join an amateurs' team and play baseball again soon. Yeah, that would fun and good exercise. He figured Zoey and Charlie would enjoy coming to his games.

Suddenly there was a loud banging on his door. What the hell? Who could that be? Logan had already made sure the outer doors of Casa Pacifica were locked, both front and back. He was still holding the baseball bat in his hand when he opened the door. Two men were standing there. Logan glanced to his right and saw that the lock on the front door to Casa Pacifica likely had been picked. The door was wide open.

A large, heavily muscled man roughly pushed open Logan's door all the way and shoved him back into his apartment. Right behind him was the man in the tan suit. Logan recognized him immediately as the man in the photo that Cass had shown him.

"You are the apartment manager?" the man Cass referred to as Ahmad demanded.

"Yes."

Ahmad retrieved a small pocket pistol from his front pants pocket. "Drop the baseball bat."

Logan complied. "What do you want?"

"Do you have a woman living here named Dylan Scott?"

"Sorry. One of my jobs is to protect tenants' privacy. I don't give out names. I don't confirm or deny residency."

Ahmad gestured to his goon and pointed to the baseball bat.

The silent man picked up the baseball bat, and before Logan could even move an inch away, the goon smashed the bat down onto Logan's left shoulder. Before Logan hit the floor, the bat smashed into his upper left arm. Now on the floor, Logan gasped and then passed out from the intense pain. He came to just long enough to hear Ahmad and the other man go up the stairs. They went to Dylan's apartment first and, judging from the sounds, they were trashing the place.

The men were looking for that laptop, Logan realized. He groaned. His cell phone was in his left pocket. He tried to reach it. Suddenly he heard the two men smash open the door to Cass's apartment. He heard Dylan scream. He passed out again from the pain. When he came to consciousness again, there was only silence. The pain was awful. He couldn't move his injured arm at all. He tried desperately to retrieve his phone. He passed out again.

* * *

When Cass arrived at the FBI office, his friend and colleague Cory Mardon was waiting for him.

"I have some news," Mardon said.

Cass grimaced. "What?"

"The accounting firm was broken into last night. The place was trashed. Obviously they were looking for something. That laptop, no doubt."

Cass nodded. He handed the laptop over to Mardon. "Here it is."

Mardon took a few steps to another desk and handed the laptop to another FBI agent, this time a woman. "Our computer forensics gal will get started right away. Also here's a bit of additional information. We learned that Ahmad Ahmad's dad served as a Saudi diplomat in Mexico for a while. Ahmad spent part of his growing up years in Mexico. He's fluent in Arabic, English, and Spanish."

Cass heard his cell phone ding. He looked at the message.

Logan had finally managed to get his phone out of his pocket. He texted Cass, using only one hand.

Dylan abducted. I'm injured. Need help.

Cass answered. *Coming now.*

Cass turned to Cory Mardon. "Shit's going down now. They took Dylan, and they attacked and wounded the apartment manager, Logan Reid. I'm going now. I have to find her."

"I'm going with you." Mardon was reaching into his desk for his gun. "I'm tired of sitting around this office. I'd like to see a little action."

"I could use some help. Let's go."

Twelve minutes later Cass and Cory arrived at Casa Pacifica. They went directly to Logan's apartment where they found Logan lying on the floor. Cass helped him sit up.

"I'll call an ambulance," Cory said.

"Tell me what happened." Cass sat on the floor next to Logan.

"Two of them. One was that man Ahmad in the photo that you showed me. His bodyguard smashed my arm and shoulder with the baseball bat. Then they went upstairs. Went first to Dylan's apartment and then to yours. They broke in. I heard Dylan screaming. They took her."

"What the hell is going on?" Frida Villarreal said. She was standing in Logan's doorway.

Cass turned to her. "Two criminals broke in, attacked Logan and abducted Dylan. Cory called an ambulance. Can you stay with Logan until the ambulance comes?"

"Yes, of course. I'll go with him if they let me. Help me get Logan on the sofa so he'll be more comfortable."

"Looks like a dislocated shoulder and probably a broken humerus bone," Mardon said. He helped Frida move Logan.

"Frida, please call my department and tell them I can't teach this afternoon." Logan's face was white. "Text Zoey, too."

"Sure. Just take a deep breath. You look like you're about to pass out, Logan," Frida said.

"We have to go, Frida," Cass said. "I have to find Dylan before they kill her."

"Oh, my god. I'll stay here with Logan. The ambulance won't take long. I'll let Zoey know what's going on." She sat next to Logan on the sofa. "You're white as a sheet, Logan. Want anything? Some water?"

Logan shook his head. He turned to Cass. "Find her, Cass."

"I will. Come on, Mardon. Let's go hunting."

* * *

Cass and Cory Mardon jumped into Cass's car.

"Where are we going?" Mardon asked.

Cass was already driving away from the apartments. "Cory, I don't know for sure where they took Dylan. But I figure the location is most likely that old ranch house and barn off a dirt road in Sahuarita where Ahmad was running those dog fights. I don't think he would try to take her across the border because the chances of getting stopped are risky. He probably has a luxury condo somewhere in the Tucson area, but he would attract too much attention if he tries to take Dylan there. She's not going to cooperate." He shook his head. "I hope she doesn't get hurt. Sometimes she doesn't know when to keep her mouth shut."

"That ranch house makes sense," Mardon said. "We found out during our investigation that Raul Ortega is the owner of that property. Or Ahmad Ahmad. Whatever his name is. We went in, arrested everyone there, and hauled off all those dogs to the rehab center in Phoenix. That means the place is isolated and abandoned now. I bet Dylan's boss is there as well."

"Yeah, if he's still alive." Cass struggled to stay calm. "If Ahmad hurt or killed Bob Hutchins, then Dylan could be next." The idea that Dylan might be hurt was more than he could bear.

"I'm calling this in," Mardon said. "FBI and the cops will be right behind us." He pulled his cell phone out. "I have my gun on me now."

"I'm carrying, too."

Cass drove as fast as possible away from the narrow streets of the Iron Horse neighborhood, onto the highway out of the city, and into the nearby town of Sahuarita. He slowed down in the residential neighborhood that he and Dylan had passed through on their way to the dog fight. When he turned onto the dirt road that led to the old ranch house, he drove slowly and finally stopped.

"Let's go on foot the rest of the way," Cass said.

Sure enough, as soon as they topped a small rise, they could see a luxury Rolls Royce parked at the front door of the ranch house. The barn door where the dog fights had been held was open.

Cass and Mardon crept along the side of the house toward the open barn door. Shadows crossed the entrance, and the two men were able to enter the barn without being seen. They could hear voices in the ring where the dog fights had been held. Both men pulled out their guns. They inched along in the shadows until they could see what was going on in the ring.

Ahmad was standing next to Dylan, his hands thrust into his suit jacket pockets. His bodyguard thug was off to the side watching. Dylan was sitting in a rickety wooden chair, her hands bound in front of her. Cass could see a cut and bruise on her cheek. She had a look on her face that could be described as both terrified and furious. Sitting next to her in another old wooden chair was a man, also bound, and also looking terrified. Bob Hutchins, Cass assumed.

Cass and Mardon exchanged glances, then nods. They stepped out of the shadows and took the classic law enforcement stance, both feet apart, arms extended and holding their guns with both hands.

"Step back. Get on the ground!" Cass shouted loudly. He heard Dylan whimper, "Shadow Man!"

Ahmad looked at Cass, smiled, and pulled a gun out of one of his pockets. He held it to Dylan's temple.

Cass fired his gun. Ahmad fell to the dirt floor of the barn, blood oozing from a hole in his chest. The bodyguard had his gun out now, and he pulled the trigger.

Mardon returned fire, and the thug hit the ground. Mardon's bullet had gone into the man's shoulder. But the thug wasn't done. He fired wildly. The first bullet flew past Mardon's head. The second went into Cass's chest. Cass heard Dylan scream as he fell to the barn's dirt floor.

Mardon kicked the thug's gun away, pulled out his phone and called for an ambulance. He went to Cass.

"How bad?"

"Bad. I need help." He could hear Dylan demanding to be untied.

Mardon quickly untied Dylan, and she ran to Cass's side. She knelt down on her knees and tore off the long-sleeve shirt that covered her tank top. She gathered her shirt into a ball and pressed the wound in an attempt to stop the blood flowing from the bullet hole in Cass's chest. Tears were streaming down her face.

"I'm okay. I'm okay," Cass whispered.

"You're *not* okay! If you die, I'm going to kill you," she growled.

Cass wanted to laugh but, before he could, his eyes rolled back in his head, and he lost consciousness.

10. Changes

Logan sat in a wheel chair in the waiting room at the hospital. His upper arm had a plaster cast on it, and the entire arm was in a sling with a strap that held his folded arm close to his body. Earlier, the doctor had given him some pain medication, and he was feeling drowsy. He looked up at the sound of Charlie's voice.

"Daddy!" Charlie started to run toward him, but Zoey grabbed his hand and pulled him back.

"Remember what I said about going slowly and not banging into your daddy?"

"Oh, yeah." Charlie stayed close to Zoey as they approached Logan.

"Hi, Charlie. Hi, Zoey." He looked up at her and smiled.

Charlie approached slowly.

"Give me a hug, son. But on this side. This arm is not hurt." Logan extended his uninjured arm and pulled Charlie to him. Charlie put his arms around Logan's neck and kissed his dad on the cheek.

"Ready to go home?" Zoey asked.

"Yes, definitely."

"You have to stay in this wheelchair until we get you outside. My car is parked in front."

She pushed the wheelchair with Logan in it, and Charlie held his hand as they made their way to Zoey's car.

Logan maneuvered himself into the back seat. Fifteen minutes later, Zoey parked in front of Casa Pacifica apartments, and Logan managed to get himself out of her car. His shoulder had begun to ache a little bit. He could feel the place where his arm had been broken. It would be aching very soon.

Zoey helped Logan get settled on the couch.

"I guess I probably can't have a beer, right?"

"Not a good idea," Zoey answered. "Alcohol doesn't go well with painkillers."

"Too bad."

"I guess I could open a bottle and you could take a sip or two, no more."

"Yes, please."

Zoey fetched a bottle of beer and opened it. Charlie sat nearby, a worried look on his face.

"Tell me about Cass," Logan said.

"He was in surgery until about an hour ago. Now he's in a post-surgery recovery room. Then they'll move him to a private room. Dylan will be with him there. She said the docs say he did well in the surgery. They expect a full recovery."

"That's good. I've been worried about him."

"You can worry about yourself now, Logan. It's time to think of yourself and your own recovery. Charlie and I are going to help you."

"Okay."

"First, we're going to have an anatomy lesson. Charlie has been confused about what has happened. You and I can help him understand."

"What should I do now?"

Zoey leaned over and kissed him on his cheek. "Wait one moment, please." Zoey went to the table and came back with some papers. "Charlie, remember when we were entomologists and studied insects?"

"I remember."

"Then we were herpetologists and studied lizards. Then we were ornithologists, and we studied birds."

Charlie nodded. "Birds are my favorite."

"Really?" Logan said. "That's good news. I like birds, too."

"Today we're going to be anatomists. We're going to study human anatomy, specifically your daddy's anatomy." She looked at Logan, grinned, and wiggled her eyebrows.

Logan was surprised. She's flirting with me, he said to himself. Oh, wow.

Zoey held up two papers with illustrations on them. "Charlie, this is the human shoulder. As you can see, this kind of ball shape is called a rotator cuff, and it fits into this socket." She pointed to the illustration. "But when it's dislocated...dislocated means it is moved from its regular location...when it's dislocated, it isn't in the socket anymore. Your daddy's rotator cuff was dislocated. The doctors pushed the rotator cuff back into place. These two parts are also called ball and socket."

"Did that hurt, Daddy?"

"Yes, it hurt a lot."

"Your daddy will have to have ice packs on it for a while, and also take some pills for the pain."

Charlie nodded. "I'm sorry, Daddy."

"I'll get better. Don't worry."

Zoey pulled the second paper out and held it up. "Notice that the rotator cuff is attached to this long bone? This is his upper arm bone, also called a humerus bone. Your daddy's humerus bone was broken into two big pieces."

"Really? I didn't know that." Logan grimaced.

"Yes, I saw the X-ray. Complete break. One of the nurses showed it to me. The nurse is the mother of one of my students. The X-ray showed that two parts of the broken bone were at least two inches apart." She held up her hands with one index finger pointing up and the other pointing down. "See, Charlie, these are supposed to be one bone." She moved her index fingers together, the finger tips touching each other. "But in the X-ray, they looked like this." She separated the fingers apart. "The doctors put the two broken parts back together." She moved her index fingers to touch each other again. "The doctors put a cast on his arm to hold the bones in place so the two broken parts can grow together again."

Charlie frowned. "That hurts, too, Daddy?"

"Yes."

"Daddy, I'm going to help you. If you want something, tell me and I'll go get it for you."

"Thank you."

Charlie nodded. "I'll bring you some toys. They will make you feel better. Especially Elmo. He's my favorite."

"Thank you. And thanks for the anatomy lesson, Zoey."

"Daddy, why did that bad man hit you with the baseball bat?"

Logan sighed. "That's hard to explain. The man who hit me did that because his boss told him to hit me. The boss was a bad guy who loves money more than he loves people."

"That's stupid," Charlie said.

"I'm going to get us something to eat for supper," Zoey said. "Charlie, please set the table."

Charlie went off to the kitchen to get the dishes.

Zoey leaned over and said in a low voice, "I'm staying here with you tonight, Logan. I'm going to take care of you."

Logan didn't know what to say. So sweet.

"I'll sleep on the couch. Then I'll get Charlie some breakfast and walk him to school."

Logan took her hand. "I'm so grateful for all your help. Perhaps I can begin making it up to you, starting with our date on Saturday night."

"We're still going on a date?" She was surprised. "Are you sure you're not too hurt?"

"Yes, I can handle it. We're going to an outdoor concert. All we have to do is sit and listen to the music. Easy." He grinned.

"A concert? Really? Who's playing?"

"Calexico."

"Oh, wow. I love Calexico!"

"Good. I want my girlfriend to enjoy herself on our date."

"I'm your girlfriend?" Zoey seemed both surprised and very pleased.

"Yes. You're my girlfriend, and we're going on a date. I hope you won't be disappointed if I can't dance, though. But I'm not much of a dancer anyway."

"That's okay. We can dance another time, but only if you want to."

"We'll have more dates. I really want to know you better because I really, really like you."

"I more than like you, Logan. I've had a huge crush on you since we first met. Remember when you said you were a grump? I fell for you then."

Logan nodded. "I thought you were very beautiful when we first met. And sweet. I think I've been enamored with you all this time, but I was afraid to say so. I didn't really know how to handle my feelings. Typical male bullshit, I guess. I need to get over myself."

"I know. I understand. It's okay."

Logan nodded. "So we agree. We'll go see Calexico, Charlie will get to play with the babysitter and her dog, and all will be well."

Zoey leaned forward and kissed him. "Logan, my boyfriend."

Charlie yelled from the kitchen. "I can't find the forks."

"Look on the dish drainer," Zoey called back.

She leaned forward and kissed Logan again. He grabbed her with his uninjured arm and kissed her right back. A long, intense kiss.

Zoey stood and headed to the kitchen. "I'm coming, Charlie. I'll help you."

Logan sat on the sofa, his arm and shoulder aching slightly, his heart full of anticipation of what was to come.

* * *

Cass tried to open his eyes. Not easy. Something was wrong. He tried again, a fluttering movement. Just enough to let some light in. Then his eyes opened, slightly wider this time. He was lying on his back looking at the ceiling. It was a pale ivory color. His chest hurt. Where the hell was he? His mind was a blank. He couldn't remember anything so he closed his eyes again.

Time passed. Now, when he woke, his eyes opened more easily, and he could feel something warm in his hand. He moved his hand and his fingers, trying to determine where the warmth was coming from. The warmth squeezed his hand.

Dylan's face appeared in front of him.

"Hi," she said softly.

"Hi," Cass whispered.

"How are you?"

"I'm okay. Where am I?" His voice sounded weak, even to him.

"In the hospital."

"Water. I need water."

Dylan disappeared. She returned with a cup and straw. She placed the straw between his lips.

"Just a little sip," she said.

Cass was incredibly thirsty. He wanted to drink every drop, but she wouldn't let him. She pulled the straw away after one sip.

"More," he croaked.

"Two more sips. Then you take a little break."

"You're a tyrant." He took two more sips.

Dylan giggled. "Oh, my love, you have no idea what a tyrant I am. You have to do what I say now."

He couldn't help himself. He smiled. "I always do what you say."

"No, you don't," she laughed. "You do what you damn well please most of the time. But now you're going to start doing what I say because I'm going to take care of you so you can get better really fast. You had surgery to remove a bullet from your chest so you've been out of it since yesterday."

"You've been here all this time?"

"No. They made me go home yesterday evening, but I came back this morning."

"What happened? I can't remember."

Dylan recounted events right up to his removal from the old ranch house by the ambulance EMTs.

"I shot Ahmad?"

"Yep, he was going to shoot me in the head so you took him out. You saved my life, Cass. He's not dead, by the way. He was severely wounded, and he has a chest wound, just like you. He and his thug were arrested. Ahmad is in the hospital under police guard."

Cass was quiet for a moment. "Okay. I remember. What about Logan?"

"Dislocated shoulder and a badly broken humerus bone in his arm. He's got a cast now, and his arm is in a sling. He was released from the hospital ER yesterday evening."

"He went home?"

"Yes. Zoey took him home, and now she's taking care of both Charlie and Logan. Charlie is trying to help. Zoey said he keeps putting stuffed toys on Logan's chest to make him feel better."

"Do I need a toy?" He looked into her eyes.

"I'm your toy! You can play with me as much as you want when you get out of here."

"Soon I hope. Can I have some more water? Please."

Dylan chuckled. "Sip slowly."

"Yes, ma'am." He sipped, this time four sips.

She put the cup down. "Are you hungry?"

"Not really."

"When you get hungry, tell me, and I'll get you something to eat."

Cass looked into her beautiful green eyes. "Dylan, I'm fed up. I'm sick and tired of getting shot."

"We're changing your life, Shadow Man. I told your friend Cory that it's a big goodbye to the FBI. No more shooting at, and, especially, no more getting shot at. It's horses twenty-four seven from now on."

Cass nodded. "Good. I've been thinking that it's time for me to leave law enforcement. I miss Betty. And Tornado."

"Betty misses you. She says for you to be a good boy and do what I tell you to do. Tornado says he wants to go for a run again."

He sighed. "I'm so glad you're not hurt."

"Me, too. Thank you, Shadow Man, for rescuing me and Bob."

"Where is your boss now?"

"Out on bond. He hired a lawyer."

Cass nodded.

"Your mom is outside in the hallway waiting to see you. I gave her a pillow, and the last time I looked, she was napping."

"She came all the way from the rez?"

"You're her son. Of course she came. She asked me some questions."

Cass looked confused. "About what?"

"She wanted to know if I love you. I said yes. Then she wanted to know if you love me. I said yes. I think so, anyway."

"I do. I love you."

"Then she wanted to know if I was going to have your children. You know? You get me pregnant, and I give birth to your babies."

"What did you say?"

"I said yes, of course. You and I are going to make a family. You, me, and a bunch of spoiled little Apache brats." Dylan shrugged her shoulders. "Well, maybe two little Apache brats. Or three."

Cass smiled. "I like the sound of this. Horses and Apache brats."

"Yeah. We'll have fun, Shadow Man." She took a deep breath. "And dogs. I like dogs."

"Horses, dogs, and Apache brats. Good."

"Oh! I have some news. I'm Native American."

Cass smiled. This should be interesting, he thought to himself. "Tell me."

"I called my dad and asked him about our family's history. He told me that my great-great-grandmother on his mother's side of the family was a member of the Shawnee tribe."

"So that makes you Native American?" He tried not to laugh. He didn't want his chest to hurt. Or hurt her feelings.

"Yes, smarty pants. Well, a little bit Native American. Better than nothing."

Cass nodded. "I'll go along with that."

"Okay, I'm going to go get your mom. You can have ten minutes with her."

"You're a tyrant."

"Shut up." She kissed him again.

Dylan left the room, and two minutes later, his mom came in.

"Hi, Mom."

The older woman smiled. She flipped her long, dark braid back over her shoulder, leaned over and kissed him on the cheek. "Dylan says I can have ten minutes." She laughed. "I approve of her. She will keep you in line. And she's going to give me some grandbabies. Just what I want. A good woman for my son. And grandbabies."

"Glad you approve. Can I have some water?"

"Only a couple of sips." She reached for the cup and straw.

Cass sighed. He sipped. His mother held his hand in affectionate silence for several minutes.

"I'm going to go get my grandbabies' mama to stay with you. I have to go home and feed the animals. Now you get well, son, and then come home to the rez soon. Be sure to bring Dylan with you."

As soon as she left his room, Cass lifted his head and looked at the cup of water. Still two thirds full. He reached for it, brought it to his lips, and drank down all the water in three big gulps. He put the cup back, dropped his head back on the pillow, and closed his eyes. A smile grew on his face.

* * *

Two weeks later, Logan turned to his son and said, "Charlie, I have an important job for you."

"A job?" Charlie looked up at his daddy and smiled. "I like jobs."

"That's good to know. Okay. Here's the job. Go to these apartments: Zoey's apartment, Li's apartment and Frida's apartment. Knock on the door. When they come to the door, tell them that Cass is home from the hospital. We're going to have Sunday potluck dinner at Cass's apartment. Tell them to come at the regular time and bring food."

"Okay!" Charlie grinned and ran for the door.

"Be polite. Don't bang on the door."

"I'll be polite." Charlie left, a grin on his face. Fifteen minutes later he was back. "Daddy, I told everyone. They are all bringing food. Zoey gave me a hug and a kiss."

"That's because Zoey is sweet, and she loves you. Thank you, Charlie. Now go to Cass's apartment. Ask Dylan if they need any help."

Charlie ran for the door again. Five minutes later, he was back. "Dylan says we need ten buckets of ice cream." He collapsed into giggles. "Just kidding."

Logan shook his head and sighed. He smiled at his smart ass son. "Okay. Thank you for all the help. I have some ice cream, two half-gallons, and we can take that along with this dish I made. It's a curry. Remember Gwilym, the Canadian? He taught me how to make curry. I'll need for you to help me carry the food upstairs. Now go find something to do until it's time to go." Logan carefully stirred the curry with his uninjured arm and hand. He still wore the sling, and his upper arm was still in a cast. The doctor had told him it would be at least two more weeks before the cast came off.

An hour later, everyone had gathered at Cass's apartment on the second floor. Cass was dressed in his regular clothing, jeans and a long-sleeve shirt, and he was resting on the sofa with his head and shoulders propped up by a pile of pillows. He greeted everyone with a big smile and hello. Dylan sat near him, a watchful look on her face.

Instead of sitting and eating at the dinner table as usual, everyone got a plate and then sat in a circle near Cass. With Dylan's help, he was able to sit up and eat along with them.

Once everyone had finished, Logan spoke.

"I know we've had a tough time here the last few months. Li was shot, Nina and Zoey, and then Dylan, were assaulted, and Cass was seriously wounded. But I think things are getting better now."

"Don't forget yourself, Logan. You were hurt, too," Zoey said.

Logan nodded. "Getting hit by a baseball bat seems like small stuff compared to a gunshot wound."

Cass shook his head. "Don't underestimate your injury, Logan."

"Okay," Logan said. "I'll add my name to the list. But, as I said, things are getting better now. I have some news. I interviewed for a teaching job at the community college, and the interview went well. So if they hire me, I'll be able to continue providing Charlie with ice cream. He won't starve."

Charlie clapped his hands. "Yay!"

"Nina and Gwilym called. They are doing well. They won't be back until September, except for a really quick weekend trip that I'll tell you about in a minute." Logan paused. "Charlie is playing softball now. Looks like he may make a good catcher. And I have a girlfriend. Her name is Zoey Corban." He leaned down and kissed Zoey who was sitting next to him. Zoey blushed. "Does anyone else have any news?"

Dylan looked at Cass. "Want to tell them what we're up to?"

"With pleasure," Cass said. "Dylan and I will be leaving Casa Pacifica soon. We're moving back to the rez, and we'll live on the acreage where I grew up. My mom is moving in with my brother's family. He and his wife have six kids, and my mom is going to help them out because both my brother and his wife have day jobs. They really need her help. Dylan and I are starting a new business. Dylan can fill you in on all the details."

Dylan nodded. "We'll run a horse farm. We plan to offer what's called 'equine therapy' for disabled and autistic kids, and for vets of traumatic events like war, fires, floods, and other disasters, whatever happens that causes trauma and PTSD symptoms. We'll be working with certified therapists skilled in this area. Also, I'll work two days a week as an accountant for local businesses. We're taking my horse Betty with us."

"And we just bought a new horse," Cass added. "His name is Tornado. He's going to live with us on the rez. We'll be adding more horses."

Everyone smiled. Thumbs up.

"We'll miss you," Zoey said.

"We won't be far away so we can come back to visit," Dylan replied. "Oh, here's another bit of good news. When we went to see that dog fight...remember I told you about that?...there was this black-and-white dog that was badly injured. The fight organizers just threw him away. When the fight ring was busted, the dog was rescued and sent to rehab. He's done really well there. He's going to live with us, too. I already spent some time with him, and I found him to be a real sweetie. I don't have a name for him yet, but we'll think of something."

Charlie jumped up and squealed, "Me! Me! Me!"

Dylan looked at him, confused. "You?"

"Name him Charlie," he giggled.

Everyone laughed.

Dylan looked over at Cass. He smiled and nodded.

"Sounds good to me," Dylan said. "We have a new dog, and his name is Charlie."

Charlie gave Dylan a hug.

"So this all means we're going to have a reorganization of the living arrangements here at Casa Pacifica," Logan continued. "Nina and Gwilym decided that they don't need a big, two-bedroom apartment. So they are making a quickie trip back to Tucson, and they will be moving Nina's stuff into Dylan's apartment. Dylan and Cass will be gone by then to their new home. So that means I will be looking for a new tenant for Nina's old apartment, Cass's now. If you have any suggestions, let me know."

"One more thing," Cass said. "Dylan and I are getting married."

Dylan grinned. "I'm marrying Cass because he needs someone to tell him what to do."

Cass shook his head and smiled. He turned to everyone and said, "So I guess this means everyone at Casa Pacifica will be invited to our wedding. It will mean a weekend trip to the Fort Apache reservation."

Everyone called out their congratulations.

Logan continued, "Here's my last bit of news. I heard from Marc. He'll be back soon, in a couple of weeks, and he still plans to bring that big dog with him. So that's about it. Charlie and I are going back to our place now because it's Charlie's bedtime. See you all next week."

Everyone said goodnight and returned to their apartments.

Dylan turned to Cass. "Shadow Man, it's time for you to take off your clothes and go get in bed."

Cass pulled her to him and kissed her. "You're such a tyrant."

Thank you from the Author:

Hello Reader!

Thank you for reading *Shadow Man*, the second Iron Horse Mystery. Please leave a review of this book wherever you buy books (Amazon, Kobo, Nook, Apple, etc.) and also at Bookbub and Goodreads. By leaving a review for others to read, you can make it much easier for mystery readers everywhere to find this book. Thank you so much. Please sign up for my monthly newsletter all about art, books, and the natural world at www.cjshane.com/contactnewsletter.html

In *Shadow Man*, Logan asks Zoey out on a date to go see and hear Calexico, a very popular indie rock group in Tucson. Interested in Calexico's music? Try this link from KEXP radio in Seattle. https://www.youtube.com/watch?v=eXzeWeAGezg The song is "Cumbia de Donde."

Apaches in Arizona

Several Apache tribes have lived in the American Southwest, the southern Great Plains, and northern Mexico for well over one thousand years. Today, federally recognized Apache tribes are found in the states of Arizona, New Mexico, and Oklahoma. Six of these nine Apache tribes are located in Arizona. Apache are also in northern Mexico in several states, among them Sonora and Chihuahua.

Apache tribes fought against the Spanish, Mexicans, and later U.S. invaders into their traditional lands. In what came to be known as the Apache Wars, the tribes fought against U.S. Army troops and also American settlers, primarily in the late nineteenth century. The Apache came to be known as skilled horsemen and fierce warriors who often engaged in raids and ambush warfare.

Apache names are still common in the American Southwest. Apache County is located in northern Arizona, and Cochise County, in the southeastern corner of Arizona, is named after Cochise, an Apache warrior and chief of the Chiricahua Apache tribe. The Chiricahua Mountains are located in southeastern Arizona as well.

The two largest Apache tribes in Arizona are the White Mountain tribe and the San Carlos tribe. Our hero in *Shadow Man,* Cass (Cassadore) Cosay, is an enrolled member of the White Mountain Apache tribe. Cass

Cosay was born and grew up on the Fort Apache Indian Reservation, which is located central-eastern Arizona.

In recent years, a controversy has broken out on the Fort Apache Reservation. Oak Flat, an area in the Tonto National Forest in the southern part of the reservation, is considered by tribal members to be sacred. Oak Flat is an important location for Apache religious ceremonies, including the Sunrise Dance, a four-day coming-of-age ceremony for girls of the tribe.

Oak Flat came under threat when a copper deposit was discovered on Oak Flat in 1994. Despite Apache efforts to stop the mining and to preserve their sacred lands, the U.S. government transferred this area in 1994 to Resolution Copper, a company owned by the Australian company Rio Tinto.

Resolution Copper has a plan to build a copper mine that would create a two-mile wide, nearly 1,000 feet deep crater at Oak Flat. This would essentially destroy the sacred Apache land of Oak Flat. The mine will also negatively affect the ecosystem of the area, including wildlife and plant life. There are also deep concerns about the mine having a negative effect on water resources in the area due to large amounts of water usage by mining, and a toxic waste dump produced by mining.

Resolution Copper insists that it is a "myth" that the mine will destroy Oak Flat.
https://resolutioncopper.com/myth-and-facts/

A lawsuit was filed to stop the mining of Oak Flat. However, the Ninth Circuit Court in a 6-5 ruling failed to protect Oak Flat. The ruling allows Resolution Copper to go ahead with its plan. The Apaches appealed this decision to the U.S. Supreme Court on September 11, 2024. As the time of this writing, the Court has not yet made a final decision.

Find out more about this lawsuit at Becket Law.
https://www.becketlaw.org/case/apache-stronghold-v-united-states/

Tribal members speak for themselves about Oak Flat.

Apache sacred land threatened by mining in Arizona. This video includes Sunrise Ceremony information and an illustration of what will happen to the Oak Flat land. https://www.youtube.com/watch?v=Zh68xOnoB_8

The Apache stronghold defending sacred Oak Flat land from a copper mine
https://www.youtube.com/watch?v=vCIGlvoxu_U

Iron Horse Next in Series?
In the Slips

1 Visit from the Vet

Marc Tomassone pulled himself up from his sofa, took a deep breath, and stretched his arms over his head. For most of the night, he'd tossed and turned. He hadn't fallen asleep until about four a.m., and now he was awake at seven, still tired. More than tired. He admitted to himself that he was exhausted, both physically and mentally. The jet lag from such a long flight made things even worse. He knew the physical exhaustion would go away with enough sleep. If he could sleep, that is. The mental exhaustion seemed to hang on like a dark cloud. He shook his head. He was going to have to find a way to get over all the things he'd seen during the nearly a year he'd worked as a photo-journalist in war zones.

He looked over at the big dog curled up into a ball in her dog crate. The door to the crate was open, but she didn't make any effort to come out. Her eyes were open, watching him. Marc shook his head. He'd tried his best to make her feel comfortable and safe with him, but nothing seemed to work. She trembled when he came near.

Marc sighed. What the hell was I thinking? he asked himself. Bringing a dog home all the way from North Africa by way of Spain? Totally nuts. He headed for the kitchen, and he made a big pot of black coffee. Strong black coffee. He looked back at the dog while he sipped the coffee. She was a big dog, a greyhound, mostly white with large rust-brown patches on her back. When he put her on the airplane, he'd learned that she weighed sixty pounds. She had big beautiful brown eyes, even when they were full of fear.

"I'm going to give you a name, and I'm going to teach you how to navigate the stairs."

The dog blinked.

Marc's apartment was on the second floor of a Spanish Revival-style home nearly one hundred years old. Some fifty years earlier, it had been remodeled and transformed into an apartment building with seven units, and then it was given the name Casa Pacifica Apartments. Casa Pacifica was located in the Iron Horse neighborhood of Tucson. Going up and down either the front or back staircase was required to get to his apartment. But the dog apparently didn't know how to climb stairs. Marc had discovered that when he had arrived home late last night. She'd stood at the bottom of the stairs, trembled, and pulled against the leash when he tried to lead her up the stairs. He'd already brought her crate in, leaving her in the car for a few minutes. Now it was her turn. There they were at the bottom of the stairs, and she wouldn't go up. So Marc carried her up. The dog went directly to her crate and curled into a ball.

Now it was early morning and a new day.

"You probably need to go out, don't you?" Marc said to the dog. He approached the crate, slipped a light-weight leash around her neck and gently pulled her out of the crate. The dog followed along with Marc as he left the apartment and walked to the stairs leading down to the first floor. But when they arrived at the stairs, immediately the dog began pulling against the leash. She refused to go down the stairs.

"Oh, good grief. You've never seen stairs before? So no up? And no down? Okay. Okay." Marc picked up the trembling dog, carried her down the stairs, and took her out into the fenced backyard of the apartment building. The dog did her thing, peeing and pooping. Then she retreated to the fenced corner, sat down, and watched him with worry in her eyes. Marc had to go pick her up again and carry her back upstairs where she went immediately into her crate. She never stopped trembling.

"I guess you've seen things and experienced things that were probably on a par with what I've seen and experienced the past year or so. I think you're traumatized. Me, too. But I'm going to make things better for both of us. I'm on a path now to live a quiet life, and I'm going to give you a quiet life, too." The dog put her head down on her front paws. She kept her eyes on him.

Marc sighed. It was good to be home. He'd grown up in Tucson, and he felt safe here. He felt safe in his apartment, too. So it's late April now, he said to himself, and it's going to be getting hot again soon. That's okay. He was back in his apartment, in his neighborhood, and among friends again. Yes, he felt safe here.

In the kitchen, Marc found an old metal pan and filled it with water. He had a small pouch of dog kibble and put that out on a paper plate. He put the water and dog food on the kitchen's tile floor. "You can have a drink and something to eat without me watching you," he said to the dog. Marc looked the other way. The dog didn't move.

"Okay. I get it. I'm going to go see Logan now. You can eat in secret."

Marc went downstairs to Logan Reid's apartment and knocked on the door. Logan, the Casa Pacifica apartment manager, opened the door almost immediately.

"Hey! Marc! You're home!" Logan reached out and gave Marc a quick hug.

"Yes, I came in late last night. Didn't want to wake you."

"Daddy! I can't find my backpack," Logan's five-year-old son, Charlie, called out from his bedroom.

Logan turned and said, "You left it in the bathroom. Hurry up or you'll be late to school." He turned back to Marc. "Kindergarten calls. I'll be gone most of the day doing university stuff. I'm sorry about that because I'd like to catch up with you."

"No problem. I'm not going anywhere so there's no hurry. We can catch up later."

"Sure. Did you bring that dog?"

"Yeah, you can meet her later."

"Charlie is very interested in meeting her. He likes dogs."

Just at that moment, Charlie appeared.

"Looks who's here. It's Marc," Logan said to his son.

Charlie looked at Marc and frowned. "I remember you. Sort of."

Marc grinned. "I've been gone a long time, but I bet you will remember me eventually. And you! You look like you've grown about foot!"

Charlie giggled. "Not that much." He stood up straighter.

"Come on, Charlie. Let's go." Logan turned to Marc. "I'll check in with you later. I'm glad you made it home safely."

"Me, too. Talk to you later."

Marc went back to his apartment. He found some more ground coffee beans at the back of his mostly-empty kitchen shelves, brewed another pot, and when the coffee had cooled, he added some milk and ice from the freezer. Nice. The rest of the coffee went into a big glass jar, and that jar went into the fridge. He looked over at the water bowl. Half the water was gone, and the dog kibble had disappeared. He chuckled.

It was good to see Logan and Charlie again. Marc had always liked Logan and how he handled his job managing the apartment building. Over time, Logan had become the friend that all the other tenants looked to for information, fair play, safety, and for camaraderie, too. Living here was really a homecoming for Marc, not just to be back in his apartment, but for the friends he'd made over time at Casa Pacifica.

He sat back on the sofa and sipped the coffee. He knew he should probably take the dog to see a veterinarian. In order to be allowed into the U.S., the dog had already been vaccinated and micro-chipped. Marc wanted to register himself locally as her owner, and have her general health checked out. Yeah, she needed to be seen by a vet. Marc moved over to a small desk, opened his laptop and began searching for veterinarians. Much to his surprise, he found a mobile vet who would come to his apartment. That seemed to be a good solution. The vet would come here, and the dog wouldn't have to experience the trauma of being in a vet's office around a lot of people and other animals. So he called and made an appointment. The receptionist said that the veterinarian, Dr. Brooks, would arrive between five and six p.m.

Marc thought about the life he'd been living. To start, he was never again going to work as a photojournalist in war zones. Yes, he wanted a new, calm, peaceful life away from the violence, away from the sound of gunshots and bombs going off, away from the sounds of children screaming. Blood everywhere. Yeah, he was going to change everything. He was ready for a peaceful life. With friends. Maybe a girlfriend. And a dog. A home. He would focus on the kind of life he was going to build for himself. First, he would do his best to improve his health. Eat well. Exercise every day. He thought about getting up early and having a run every morning. It would be especially pleasurable if he could get this dog to run with him. That's what greyhounds are known for. Running. Yeah, that's what they do. Run. He looked over at the dog. She didn't move.

"One of these days, you're going to get used to me. Eventually, you are going to decide that you like me. You'll wag your tail when you see me coming. Just you wait and see."

The worried look on her face remained the same. Marc knew that she wasn't accustomed to being spoken to. Yelled at, maybe. But not spoken to in a friendly manner. "Yes, you're going to like me one of these days. I promise." The dog blinked.

Marc went to the bathroom and stared at himself in the mirror. His dark hair was longer than usual, now a mass of soft curls that almost touched his shoulders. He needed a haircut. And a shave. He'd grown a beard when he was in the field working, shaved it off before leaving for the U.S., and now it was growing back, a shadow on his jaws and chin. Hair length and beard he could fix. But what could he do about the dark shadows under his eyes? That might take some time.

"I'll get there," he spoke out loud. "I'll make a good life for myself. And I'll make a good life for that dog. Damn it." He went back to the sofa, stretched out, and fell asleep again.

The sun was moving down in the western sky when Marc woke again. He reached for his cell phone. Nearly six p.m. The sun would go down in about forty-five minutes. He heard a soft knock on his door. Maybe that's the vet. He pulled himself up and went to the door.

When he opened it, he took a step back in surprise. Standing there was one of the most beautiful women he'd ever seen. She was African American, slender and tall, maybe five feet ten inches, with very short Afro-style hair.

She was dressed casually in khaki pants and a dark knit shirt. Large gold loop earrings hung from her ears, and a colorful beaded necklace was around her neck. Marc had a sudden urge to get his camera. She was seriously beautiful.

He realized he hadn't said anything. "Uh...can I help you?"

By this time, the woman had reached into her bag and retrieved a pin-on name tag. She attached it to her vest pocket. It read, 'Angela Brooks, D.V.M.'

Marc shook his head. "Gosh. I'm sorry. You're the vet. You just surprised me."

"Yes, I'm the veterinarian you requested. I came in my mobile unit, and you're my last call of the day." She looked vaguely annoyed.

"Oh, duh! I'm so sorry. I just woke up, I'm still jet lagged, and I'm sort of a mess. Please come in, Dr. Brooks." He stepped back and opened the door wide.

A look of sympathy replaced the annoyance. "Traveling from afar? Jet lag is tough. I know that from personal experience." Her eyes surveyed his living room and landed immediately on the dog curled up in the crate.

"Yeah, I just flew in late yesterday from Spain. Before that I was in Casablanca. That's in Morocco. And before that, Sudan and Yemen. And northern Nigeria. And Ukraine."

The veterinarian's eyebrows went up. "Whoa. I bet you have some stories to tell, Mr. Tomassone. What were you doing in all those countries?"

"Photojournalism. I was taking photos of the conflicts."

Angela nodded. She approached the crate and knelt down. "What's this beauty's name?"

"I don't know. And you can call me me Marc. That will be easier."

"Okay, Marc." She looked up at him, a question on her face. "What about the dog? You don't know her name?"

Marc winced. "She's one of my stories, Dr. Brooks. No, I don't know her name."

"We need to come up with a good name for her and use it so she'll get used to it. Has she shown any signs of aggression?"

"No," Marc said. "Actually, she seems terrified of everything. I think maybe she's spent much of her life in a crate or a cage or some kind of enclosure."

Dr. Brooks nodded. She reached out slowly with one hand and extended her fingers toward the dog's nose. The dog's nose touched her fingers, sniffed, then pulled back. Her worried gaze went from Dr. Brooks to Marc and back to the veterinarian again.

Dr. Brooks reached into her bag and pulled out a small dog biscuit. "Here you go, sweetheart," she said in a soft voice.

The dog took the dog biscuit and began crunching it.

"That's a good sign. With a treat now and then, we can convince her that we're friendly." Dr. Brooks stood up. "How do you get her to come out of the cage?"

"She doesn't have a collar so I put this leash around her neck," he gestured behind him, "and I sort of pull her out. She'll come out with a little nudging."

"That's called a slip leash. So she accepts that?"

"Yeah. She comes out then she just stands there and trembles. I have to carry her downstairs so she can go out and do her business. She doesn't know how to go up and down stairs."

"That can't be easy on you. I bet she weighs at least sixty pounds."

"Yeah. That's exactly how much she weighs. But I don't have any other option. She's too scared to navigate the stairs."

"That's sad. Please bring her out now so I can take a look at her."

Marc leashed the dog and urged her to come out. She crept out and stood there trembling.

Dr. Brooks began a slow and careful examination of the dog. She ran her hands over the dog's body, palpitated her abdomen, looked into the dog's eyes, ears and mouth, and checked her gums, too. Then the doctor pulled a stethoscope from her bag and listened to the dog's lungs and stomach. She inserted a thermometer into the dog's anus to take her temperature. Then the doctor's hands returned to the dog, stroking her while examining her joints and spine. She hesitated when she came in contact with the dog's lower right-front leg. All the time the veterinarian's hands were on the dog, Dr. Brooks spoke softly in a low voice to the dog. Marc was surprised that the dog accepted all this so easily. The vet clearly knew what she was doing.

Dr Brooks turned to Marc and asked, "You have vaccination papers, right? Dogs have to be vaccinated before they can enter the U.S."

"Yes. I have her papers. She's been micro-chipped, too."

"How did you come to meet this beauty?"

"I was heading home, and I stopped by to see a friend in Morocco. We went to the dog races. His idea. I'm not into that kind of thing normally, but he wanted to go." Marc stood up. "Turns out that for a while now, my friend has been rescuing some of these dogs from the racetrack and finding them new homes. Somehow he convinced me to adopt her. I know it's crazy." He shook his head.

The veterinarian smiled. "I bet those big brown eyes were hard to resist."

"I guess. I don't know what I was thinking. Or not thinking." Marc frowned.

"You mentioned Spain."

"Apparently my friend has found homes for several of these racing greyhounds, but he takes them to Spain first because it's easier to ship them to other European countries and to the U.S. from there. He bought this dog from the race track people, shipped her to Spain, and I met him again there in Madrid. I had to get the dog registered and vaccinated and micro-chipped to fly her to America and get her through customs and all that." He went to his briefcase and pulled out papers. He handed them to Dr. Brooks.

"I see the Spanish documents. But what about these? The text is all in French or Arabic," she said.

"Yes, these are the papers from the original owner in Morocco. I don't know either language. I guess I should get this translated into English."

"I speak and read French. This says 'Nom: Saint Guinefort.' So her name is Saint Guinefort. That's a mouthful. How about if we call her Guine for short. We could change the spelling to Gwen so people will know how to say it. Or just tell them to say 'Gwen.' Or 'Gwenny'? How about that? Gwenny? What do you think? And you can call me Angela." She smiled.

"Okay. Change her name to 'Gwenny'. Sounds good to me." Marc looked at the dog and said, "Hey, Gwenny. Dr. Brooks...uh...I mean Angela...just gave you a name. And you are standing there and accepting her examination. I bet you like her touching you like that."

While the veterinarian gently ran her hands over Gwenny's sleek body, Marc started searching on his cell phone. "Hey, Wikipedia says Saint Guinefort was a greyhound in France in the thirteenth century. The local folk thought of her as a folk saint."

"That's interesting," the doctor said.

"Gwenny, are you a saint?" Marc chuckled.

Gwenny raised her head and looked at him. She looked a tiny bit relaxed. Angela the Vet was already helping the dog with her soft strokes and soft voice.

Angela pulled out a hand scanner to check for a microchip. "Yes, Gwenny has a microchip. I'm going to register her with Pima County so you'll be on record as her owner. I need your contact information. You'll get a tag in the mail to put on her collar. You need to get a collar." She handed her cell phone to Marc, and he filled in the required information.

"So with the microchip, if she runs off, it will be easier to return her to me, right?" Marc shook his head. He wondered if Gwenny might be waiting for a chance to run away. Probably not. That would be too scary for her.

"Yes. But you need to keep her safe. No running off. She might get hit by a car." Angela sat back on the floor and looked at Marc.

"Let's sit on the sofa," Marc suggested. They moved to the sofa, and Gwenny went back to her crate.

"Here's what I've learned from this preliminary exam. Gwenny is about four years old. Her front right leg was broken at some point. I can feel where the bone broke and healed, although I would like to get an x-ray to know how bad the break was. There's evidence, too, that she's been bred."

"She's had puppies?"

"Yes, I'm pretty sure about that. Likely more than one litter."

"But I thought she was a racing dog."

"She probably was at some point," Angela said, "but her race track days may have ended when she broke her leg. If she was fast, they probably decided to breed her with a fast male and produce fast puppies."

Marc frowned. "One of the men I talked to at the track told me that the racing hounds were taken out every day for exercise. I'm wondering now if Gwenny's leg and her pregnancies meant she was stuck in a cage most of the time."

"Very likely. Her muscles are a bit on the flaccid side."

"So she's about four years old? What is that in dog years? One dog year equals seven human years, right? So four times seven is twenty-eight?"

Angela shook her head. "That's not really accurate. The size of the dog makes a big difference. Gwenny is a greyhound so she's a big girl. I'd say four years is more like forty-five in human years.

"Wow. So she's entering middle age?"

"That's right."

"I hope I can give her a better life," Marc said.

"You already are giving her a better life."

Marc felt this wave of....of what?...relief?...come over him. Maybe that's why he'd adopted her. To help her and himself get over a lot of sadness and to make a better life for them both.

"So have you been sitting here in this room and just sort of hanging out with Gwenny?"

"Yes. I'm on the sofa. She's in the crate. I don't bother her unless it's time to go outside."

"That's probably the very best thing. She's becoming accustomed to you. She knows by now that you're unlikely to hit her or yell at her."

Marc shook his head. "No way would I do that. I want her to trust me."

Angela Brooks smiled. "Look. I wonder if we could try something. I have a special interest in what's called veterinary behavioral health. It's a specialty in helping animals get over trauma and then begin to lead a more normal life. Sometimes this means dealing with aggression, but in this case, it's just the opposite. She's obviously very timid and afraid. Would you be willing for me to come by here in my off hours and work with Gwenny a little? I think I could help her get over her trauma. No charge. It would be a favor to me, actually, because I'm trying to learn more about animal behavior therapy."

Marc grinned. "Gosh, that would be great. Tomorrow? Or Sunday?"

Angela smiled. "I can't tomorrow because I'm working. But how about Sunday afternoon? That would be good for me. How about if I come around three?"

"We'll be here."

Angela stood up. "I'll see you then." She collected her equipment, turned to Gwenny and said, "Goodbye, sweetie. I'll see you Sunday." The dog's ears went up. Angela turned to Marc and said, "By the way, what does that sign on the street mean? It says 'Iron Horse District.'"

"This part of town is where the railroad executives and workers lived when the railroad first came to Tucson. That was about a hundred years ago."

"Oh, I see. The Iron Horse refers to the railroad."

"Yes, you got it." Marc followed her to the door.

Angela turned and smiled. She stuck out her hand. Marc took it. "Nice to meet you, Mr. Marc Tomassone."

Marc grinned. "My pleasure, Dr. Angela Brooks."

She turned and left, heading toward the front downward staircase.

Marc closed the door behind her, still grinning. He felt much better than he had earlier in the day. What a lovely woman. He returned to his place on the sofa and began thinking about getting something to eat for supper. Maybe Gwenny would go with him for a short walk around the neighborhood.

Suddenly Marc heard voices screaming and yelling. The sounds were coming from the front of the Casa Pacifica building. He looked over at Gwenny. Her ears were up again. She'd heard the noise, too. Marc jumped up and headed out the door, closing it behind him.

2 An Uninvited Visitor

Marc sprinted down the hallway and took the stairs down to the ground floor two steps at a time. Logan was coming out of his apartment door, and Marc heard him say, "Charlie, you stay here with Zoey." Logan closed the door behind him. Someone was coming down the stairs behind Marc. He turned and saw Li, another resident that Marc had known before he left Tucson. Logan and Li followed Marc out to the front of the Casa Pacifica apartments.

The yelling and screaming had stopped.

Standing on the sidewalk was Angela Brooks, the veterinarian. Next to her was a woman that Marc had never seen before. The two women were holding hands and staring at Angela's mini-van. Although the sun was low in the sky to the west, there was still enough light for Marc to see a sign on the side of the van. It said, "Tucson Mobile Veterinary Services." There was a graphic of a dog and a cat grinning at them.

Li was standing next to Marc now. "Hey, Marc. Welcome home."

"Hey. I just got back."

"What's going on here?" Logan said in a firm voice.

Marc took a few steps forward toward Angela. "Are you okay?"

Angela turned to him. "Yeah. Just a little shook up." She released the other woman's hand. "She helped me."

"What happened?" Logan asked....